The Cook Book

A LESLIE LARUE MYSTERY

Molly Owen

This book is a work of fiction. Names, characters, places, and incidences are products of the author's imagination or used fictitiously and are not to be construed as real. Any resemblance to actual events, locales, organizations, or persons living or dead, is entirely coincidental.

Copyright © 2020 by Molly Owen

All rights reserved. Except as permitted under the U.S. Copyright Act of 1976, no part of this publication may be reproduced, distributed, or transmitted in any form or by any means, or stored in a database or retrieval system, without the prior written permission of the author.

Printed in the United States of America.

ISBN 978-1-0878-6449-5

I dedicate this book to my 'girls' whose
Christian faith inspires me daily.

ACKNOWLEDGMENTS

Anyone who has spent time in New Orleans knows how exciting it is to pick up a menu and see the many unique dishes served in restaurants and cafés. For years my husband and I took many long weekend trips to the French Quarter. We enjoyed the atmosphere, jazz music, and wonderful food that teased our palettes. Memories of those times feed my stories that take place in New Orleans, like no place on earth it takes you away from boring and transforms your imagination. The old buildings representing many different architectures and styles take you away to places unknown. The aromas from cooking and sea air fills your nostrils.

Surrounded by waterways, swamps and the amazing Mississippi river New Orleans calls you to experience her diverse culture that includes French, Spanish, Arcadian and Native American Indians to name a few. In talking to many locals while visiting there we discovered Christians live among the many peoples and religions of NOLA.

Molly Owen

So, with that in mind, I want to thank natives of New Orleans, and especially the locales in the French Quarter, for fueling my imagination as I entertain my readers in this series of The Leslie LaRue Mysteries.

Chapter **1**

A typical tropical storm invaded the New Orleans coastline in the Gulf of Mexico greeting the Rye family as they scurried around eating breakfast, fixing lunches and finding last night's homework. Leslie put the breakfast dishes in the sink and ran a quick stream of water over them. Then pouring another cup of coffee she handed it to Sidney. He took a sip and handed it back to her.

"Ryan, get a move on. Traffic will be bumper to bumper with this downpour," Sidney called upstairs to his son who was usually running late.

"Coming, Dad. Have you seen my backpack?"

"No, Son. Where did you put it last night while you were doing your homework?"

"Oh yeah, good call. It's in the dining room. Thanks, Dad."

"No problem, now get a move on. I'll meet you in the car. Don't forget your windbreaker. It's pouring cats and dogs out there."

Ryan came running down the stairs two at a time. As his long lanky legs hit the floor, he grabbed his backpack and the lunch Leslie handed him. He was at that awkward stage causing him to bang into the kitchen counter as he headed for the back door.

"Be safe you two. Have a blessed day," Leslie called out after them from the screened door of the back porch longing for days past when life was calmer and the three of them had time to sit down and have a meal together. She missed their morning devotionals and bedtime prayers with their son.

Ryan, at thirteen years old, was becoming more irresponsible every day. Sidney told her it was his age and he would soon outgrow it. Leslie thought, as she finished cleaning up the kitchen, how it couldn't come soon enough. The more organized she got, the less organized Ryan was and by the time he was out the door on his way to school she just wanted to plop in a chair and regroup.

Just then the phone rang. Seeing it was Sidney she hurried to answer. "Sid is everything all right or did you forget something," she said with despair.

"Ryan forgot his math book. He thinks he left it on the dining room table," Sidney said with irritation in his voice. "So I'm circling back to the front so he can get it."

Leslie found the left-behind math book and took it to the front galley and waited for Ryan. Sidney stopped in front of the house and as cars drove through the rain-soaked street they splashed large waves of water to cover the car Sidney sat in, waiting for Ryan. He watched as people passed him trying to avoid being splashed as they ran to catch the streetcar. When his son got back in the car, he was wet from head to foot. His shoes sloshed with wet socks. Sidney didn't say a word but vowed to have a man to man talk with his son that evening.

Leslie watched as her men drove down St. Charles street in what appeared to be monsoon and prayed for their safety. Back in the house, she decided to wait before going outback, in the rain, to her studio. Lately, her creativity inspired a decorating project she could work on until the storm went through. So, she finished cleaning the kitchen and still in her nightclothes went upstairs to get dressed. Entering their bedroom her thoughts went to Sidney. He had been on edge the past few weeks and she wondered if it had something to do with work. He complained about being tired and seemed irritable. Usually calm and reserved, his personality was now more volatile, he seemed angry most of the time and it worried her. Standing still, she began to pray, *Heavenly Father, Your Glory surrounds our family every day. Please forgive our lack of obedience and commitment to the study of your Word. I thank you for blessing us with your love and grace, Lord. I ask safety for Sidney and Ryan today. Father, watch over Sidney, give him peace with whatever is bothering him. In Jesus' Name. Amen.*

Eventually, the storm passed and the sun lit up the world shining on the wet leaves turning them into shimmering jewels hanging on the trees. Water dripped from the roof and splashed in puddles on the ground. Leslie loved the smell after the rain washed everything clean. Finished with her decorating project, she gathered her sack lunch and thermos and headed for the studio being careful to use the stepping stones leading to the building behind the house.

Sunbeams fell across her desk beckoning her to finish the book, her twentieth, about a young couple falling in love. It reminded her of when she and Sidney fell in love and the mystery that brought them together. They would soon celebrate their fifteenth wedding anniversary. She hoped the sunshine would help Sidney's mood when he returned home after getting Ryan from school. She had offered to pick him up herself but Sidney told her he would get him.

Her fingers were flying across the keys as her mind churned up one thought after another. The flow of the words brought excitement. She loved it when the story came together almost effortlessly. Interrupted by the ringing of her cell phone she glanced at the number on the screen, seeing who it was answered it.

"Hi, Annabelle. How are things in your world?" she asked leaning back in preparation for a long conversation with her close friend.

"What a morning. Getting two girls off to school was ridiculous. I just hope it isn't like this all year. The twins are so picky about everything from what to wear, of all things, how to fix their hair. Just comb it and let's go, I tell them every morning. Honestly, Leslie, you are so lucky to have a boy."

"Well, our morning didn't go very well either. You would think by this age they would remember where they left what and not make their Dad, who by the way was already upset with him, come back because he left his math book at home. It was right next to the backpack he took with him. So I guess we parents just have to grin and bear it. I'm sure the day will come when we will think back about all of this and be sad that they are grown up."

"You're probably right but it sure is nice to talk it out with someone who has been there. I love you, Leslie, I thank God every day for our friendship. We are kindred spirits. We are so

The Cookbook

blessed to have each other. Now let's change the subject, how is the book coming?"

"Today, it has taken on a life of its own. I love it when that happens."

"Well, I better let you get back to it. I'll talk to you later. Bye for now."

Annabelle, a local attorney, and Leslie's closest long-time friend had shared many occasions together from solving mysteries to being in each other's weddings and present at the birth of each one's children.

The afternoon sun was shining through the other windows now as it began to set in the west. Leslie stretched her shoulders rotated her neck and saving her work, she closed her laptop. Sidney and Ryan would soon be home and she needed to start dinner. She always looked forward to her family back under one roof and hoped that Sidney had a better day.

Standing in the kitchen, by the sink, she heard the car pull into the driveway. Then she heard the loud bang of a shutting car door. Ryan came through the back door and went straight upstairs not saying a word to Leslie as he dropped his backpack at the bottom of the stairs. Soon Sidney came into the kitchen and gave Leslie a kiss on the cheek then headed for his office where he put his briefcase on his desk. Drying her hands on a kitchen towel, Leslie followed him to his office and ask what happened.

"Our son doesn't like being corrected. He doesn't want to be told what to do. He is thirteen going on twenty and thinks he is capable of running his own life. I told him from now on I will be leaving on time with or without him and I will not be returning to get something he forgot. He either gets it together or he is on his own. I told him that maybe riding the streetcar

Molly Owen

with two or three transfers, across town will be his mode of transportation if he has no respect for my time and efforts."

Leslie stood in silence. She knew he was right, however, she may have handled it a little differently.

"So, was I wrong?" Sidney said red in the face, his breathing labored.

"No," she answered.

"I'm sick of his attitude, Leslie. He treats us like his slaves, ready to do or be at his beck and call. I noticed his backpack thrown at the bottom of the stairs after I told him to keep his things in his room. This will stop." He said eyes flaring.

Knowing he was upset, she didn't say anything for fear it would upset him more. This was not his normal reaction to Ryan nor for Sidney to act so rash. She went to him and put her arms around his neck and gave him a hug, then leaving him, she went back to the kitchen to finish preparing their dinner. As she washed the vegetables for the salad, she asks God to help them with parenting their son. *Almighty, Father, we give this situation to you. Be with us as we figure out the best way to work with our son. Give us the courage to discipline in love and strength to help our son grow into a fine young man. Thank you. In Jesus' name. Amen.*

She saw Sidney go to the powder room under the staircase to freshen up as she began to set the table for supper. After Leslie called upstairs to announce that dinner was ready, Ryan came down and sat at the table. Leslie set the rolls on the table as she pulled out her chair and sat down. It was then she realized that Sid was still in the powder room. Getting up from the table she went and knocked on the door. After no answer, she opened the unlocked door. Sidney wasn't in the room. She hadn't seen him leave the powder room. She looked in his office then went upstairs to their bedroom and found him sitting on a bench at the end of the bed.

"Sid, are you all right?" she said with concern.

"I'm not sure. I may be having a heart attack."

Leslie went to him and realized he was sweating profusely and white as a sheet.

"Oh, God, what do I do?" she cried out.

She reached for the phone and called for an ambulance. Then, leaving him for just a second she went to the bedroom door and called out to Ryan. He came running up the stairs two at a time and on seeing his Dad he ran to him. The fear in his eyes prompted Sidney to reassure his son that he would be okay as the sound of sirens filled the tense air around them.

Ryan rushed down the steps to the front door and let the paramedics come through with their equipment. Urgency prompted him while he led them up the stairs encouraging them to hurry. This was his father, dad, and the thought of not having him in his world overshadowed anything that had happened earlier. An awareness overcame him as he pushed thoughts of his responsibility for this back in a dark place.

An enormous amount of dread filled her as she watched the medics unbutton his shirt then remove it revealing his pale chest trying to contain the incredible pain. Beads of sweat poured from his face.

"Shouldn't he lie down?" Leslie asked with an overwhelming need to help.

One of the men calmly reassured her and continued to attach little white round sticky circles, with silver nipples in their centers, to different areas of his chest, while the other man prepared his arm with a place to insert a needle connected to a bag of fluid. Their calm efficiency permeated the room. Finally, after what seemed hours they were carefully taking him on the gurney down the stairs and out to the waiting emergency unit.

Leslie followed close behind. Before they lifted him into the back of the unit, she reached over and took his hand, bowing her head she asked God for his protection, courage, and strength. Then reluctantly releasing his hand she motioned for Ryan, standing on the sidewalk, and told him to call Annabelle to bring him to the hospital, then with the help of the paramedic climbed into the front passenger seat of the unit just as she had several years ago with Ryan after he choked on a plastic baby in a King's Cake. She reminded herself to breathe and bowing her head began to pray.

The Cookbook

Chapter **2**

For many years Leslie wrote stories of love, romance, and mysteries. Since New Orleans was a mecca of food sources including fruits, veggies, and endless amounts of fresh seafood, she decided to put the novels behind her and start writing cookbooks. Being a native of Louisiana she found the history of her heritage fascinating. She knew that not many places were as colorful in culture and cuisine as New Orleans. Spending many hours in her kitchen developing her own recipes and knowing that her genre would most likely be travels interested in the history of the cuisine in New Orleans, she decided to include some background leading up to the development of many famous dishes known for their birth in, mainly, the French Quarter.

Her cookbook was divided into two categories Cajun and Creole. She thought a little history would add to the appeal of the cookbook. For Cajun recipes, she describes them as more country home style, where they use the bounty from the land and wild game—such as alligators and crawfish—in the recipes representing farmers and trappers. Cajun cooking included what they referred to as Cajun Holy Trinity—onions, celery, and green peppers—a lot like the classic French mirepoix that uses carrots instead of green peppers.

The second half of the cookbook represented Creole cuisine, a more sophisticated city food developed using fresh seafood from the gulf, vegetables, and spices bought off the ships coming in from the islands in the Caribbean. Both Creole and Cajun foods were known for their roux. However, they were made differently, she explained. The Creole early on had the means to keep butter fresh which together with flour was the start of many spicy Creole dishes. The Cajun, on the other hand, who lived in the swamps and on farms were unable to keep butter fresh, so they used oil instead, adding flour to make their roux.

Without her son Ryan underfoot, she was able to spend more time on developing recipes for her cookbooks. Also giving her time to care for her organic garden where the many vegetables ended up in her dishes prepared for a space in her cookbooks.

Now a freshman at Tulane University, Ryan was enjoying college life, living in the dorm and preparing for a degree in criminal law.

"Mom, please don't fuss, I don't have time for you to fold my clothes. I just want them clean. I have to go, Mom. Just let me have the basket so I can leave," he begged.

"Ryan, if you fold them right out of the dryer....."

"Mom. I know. They won't wrinkle," Ryan said grabbing the clothes and stuffing them in the basket.

The Cookbook

"Okay. Give me a hug and I won't keep you any longer," Leslie said leaning in for her goodbye hug. "Thanks for helping me with the garden yesterday. It helped a lot."

"Sure. Bye, mom see you Friday," Ryan said running out the back door before she could say anything else.

Leslie sighed as she watched her son throw the basket of clean clothes in the old black pickup truck, with the paint chipping off, inherited from, Nick, his grandfather, back out of the parking space. As he drove off he waved and then he was gone.

She enjoyed time spent with Ryan and she hated to see him leave but the tug of her heartstrings was an indication for her to let go. She always pictured this time after he left his home to be both sad and happy. But now she found it hard to just let go and let him make his own choices. Ryan was more responsible than others his age and he always kept up his grades with a little nagging from his mother. He was her only child and she wanted the best for him. *Oh, Father, I need to back off and let him find himself out in the real world. We have given him a good foundation full of love, wisdom, and hope for his future now it is his time to show us he can do it on his own. Thank you, Father, for watching over him and Father help me to not interfere, and hold on too tight. Give me the strength to let go and not have it all be about me. In Jesus' Name. Amen*

In her meditation time, unwilling memories of that day over five years ago would possess her thoughts, leaving her uneasy knowing it could happen again. Her need to keep Sidney close, at times, put a strain on their marriage. He had told her, more than once, it would be God's timing and His will that would determine their future. So going forward they would live each day as their last and smell the roses along the way. For the most part, their lives had fulfilled that declaration.

Today, Sidney had gone into the French Quarter to get some fresh shrimp for the jambalaya Leslie was making for supper. Jeffrey and Annabelle were coming to help them celebrate their twentieth wedding anniversary.

Leslie went back to the kitchen and started chopping veggies to go in the jambalaya. When she took an onion out of the bin she saw an envelope addressed to "my parents." Taking a knife she slid the blade under the sealed flap. It was an anniversary card. The thought had crossed her mind earlier that Ryan had forgotten their anniversary. She pulled the handwritten card out and read it.

> *Dear Mom and Dad,*
>
> *I just want to tell you how proud I am of both of you. I am blessed to have you as my parents. I know I don't say it as often as I should but I love you both very much.*
>
> *Happy Anniversary,*
>
> *Your Son,*
> *Ryan*

Leslie's eyes welled up in tears with an appreciation for the gesture. She had learned through the years of raising this son of hers that these sentiments didn't come easy which made this hand-written card even more special. Bowing her head in prayer she thanked her heavenly Father.

The past few years found Ryan and Sidney inseparable. They went on many fishing trips together on Lake Pontchartrain in a bass boat she got Sidney for his birthday. The two of them also went to all the Saints home games and the three of them went to a couple of out-of-town games together.

The Cookbook

She and Ryan's relationship was more on the line of preparing him for the world which included teaching him self-discipline and making sure he studied hard to be able to get into the college of his choice. As it turned out, he wasn't quite ready to move away from New Orleans to attend college. So his mom's alma mater was what he settled on. Leslie was disappointed that he wasn't going to experience being out from under her continued parenting. She hoped he would go off to college, not too far away, but far enough that he couldn't come home every weekend. However, Sidney didn't see a problem with him staying close by and even encouraged Ryan to come home every Friday evening or at the latest Saturday morning.

In all their years of marriage, they tried to stay on the same page as parents. However, when Ryan was in high school participating in sports, Sidney became Ryan's advocate sometimes going against Leslie's better judgment.

When Ryan started school and after the accident when he swallowed a plastic baby out of the King's Cake on his fifth birthday, Leslie would not allow him out of her sight. Sidney accused her of smothering their little boy. Try as she might, her strong feelings of protection would take over.

Ryan put on the personality that pleased his mother, knowing she would support him no matter what. Sidney, on-the-other-hand, was more exposed to the real Ryan as they spent private time together doing guy things.

Leslie pushed Ryan to do his best and make excellent grades in school. Out of respect for his mother, he would accomplish all the things he knew she wanted from him. After his Dad's heart attack, five years ago, things changed between him and Sidney. They did fun things together and had long talks about the future. It was like Sidney was preparing him for when he was gone and Ryan would have to take care of his mother. Ryan didn't dwell on this conclusion because the thought of losing his Dad was just too painful.

*****

That night at dinner as the four friends enjoyed Leslie's jambalaya the conversation went to their kids, as it often did. The Bordeaux twins, Jeffrey's and Annabelle's only children, were now twelve and while they spent the night at Jeffrey's sister, and didn't have school because of a teachers' workday, Jeffrey and Annabelle were happy to have adult time with friends.

"The girls are doing really well in gymnastics. Their instructor, Karlah, thinks they can go to the competition held in Houston in a few weeks. We aren't sure if we are ready for that, yet. How did you two handle going out of town when Ryan played football?" Annabelle asked.

"Oh, you'll get used to it. We looked forward to it and I personally wanted to be there in case he got hurt or something," Leslie said.

"Well thanks, Leslie, I hadn't thought about that yet," Annabelle said glaring at her.

They all laughed. After dessert, the men helped to clear the table. Then the women went to see some new items Leslie had bought for the den upstairs, leaving the men to talk.

"I wanted to ask you, Sidney, how's business? Are you still watching your schedule? "

"We're still busy but we just don't take on more than we can handle. Why? You need me to look into something for you?"

"Yeah, I haven't mentioned this to Annabelle, so keep it under your hat," Jeffrey said.

"Sure. What's up"

"It's this gymnastic thing with the girls. Karlah, their instructor is having some issues with one of the fathers," he told him.

"What kind of issues?"

"She thinks he's stalking her," he said. "He hangs around her every chance he gets and follows her home in his car."

"How long has this been going on?"

"She said it began when he first started bringing his daughter to class. The mother doesn't seem to be in the picture. She doesn't know the reason for that and doesn't want to encourage anything by asking. She confided in me last week when I picked the girls up after practice. She made some excuse in front of him to talk to me privately. I told her I had a friend who could do a background check and she thanked me. So, without getting the gals involved do you think you could check it out?"

"Sure. Just give me some information on this guy and I'll run a background check on him."

"I appreciate it. She may be overreacting but she seems pretty worried. She said she just has a strange feeling around him like something isn't right. She is young, I would guess about Ryan's age. She goes to Tulane and also works at the gym. She teaches classes during the afternoon after the kids get out of school."

"Does she live alone?"

"She didn't say. Do you want me to find out?"

"No. Let's see what we find out about this guy first. I'll let you know."

"Thank you, Sidney," Jeffrey said and handed him the information.

"No problem, glad to help," Sidney said, as he looked at the name on a small piece of paper then put it in his shirt pocket.

Upstairs Leslie showed Annabelle her latest decorating project in the upstairs den.

"I love it, Leslie. Not only are you a wonderful writer but your creativity comes through in other ways. How on earth did you come up with this idea?"

"I don't know. I just wanted to do something different. The rest of the house is so Garden District, so I just decided to go more bohemian, more like the French Quarter. It isn't too much? Is It?" Leslie said arms crossed looking around the room.

"Heavens, no. It's inviting and intriguing just like the French Quarter. Full of fun and surprises. Oh, Leslie, I think it's great," Annabelle said going around the room, looking at every detail. "It reminds me of you. Unpredictable, colorful, sincere and yet mysterious. Where did you get this furniture?"

"I've been collecting it for a long time. Shopping the antique malls, estate sales. Believe it or not, that ugly piece over there came right off the curb where someone left it for the trash haulers. I thought it was calling for a bright redo, so I painted it purple," Leslie laughed.

"What does Sidney think?"

"At first he said it would take some getting used to, however, I catch him in here every once in a while. I think it calls to him. It's anything but peaceful, what with the red walls, but maybe it puts him in a different frame of mind. It's exciting and maybe that is what he needs, you know, a different kind of excitement from his daily detective work," Leslie shared with Annabelle. "It perfectly changes my mood. It's like a huge painting you get lost in."

"How is he doing? Didn't he recently have another checkup?"

"Yes. The doctor put him on another medication for stress. But other than that he is doing okay, thank God," Leslie said turning out the light as they left the room.

"Speaking of paintings, Jeffrey and I are taking a painting class together," Annabelle told Leslie as they descended down the stairs to the living room where they left the men.

"Oh, how fun. Sid and I ought to take some classes together," Leslie said going to Sidney and giving him a hug.

"Well, we better leave these people to celebrate their anniversary," Jeffrey said winking at Sidney.

*****

Later that evening as they lay next to each other in bed, Sid said a prayer out loud. *"Heavenly Father thank you for a wonderful day and time with our close friends. Thank you for my loving, patient, and impulsive, wife and bless our son in his studies. Father, we ask you to help him to stay on track. Thank you for our good health, our wonderful marriage and hope for our future. These things we pray in Jesus' Name. Amen."*

After kissing Leslie, he told her goodnight and turned out his light. She reached over and turned her light out. A couple of seconds later she turned her light back on and sat up. Sidney turned over to face her in anticipation of what she was about to say. Instead, she laid back down and turned the light off again.

"What?" he said knowing she needed to say something.

"When have I been impulsive lately?"

"Honey, you are always impulsive," he said laughing

"But, you prayed about it. So, you must have something in mind that has bothered you. So, Sid, when lately, have I been impulsive?" she said lying still in the dark waiting for his answer.

"Did you hear the part about you being lovely and patient?" he said teasing her.

"Sid, I'm serious."

"Come on Sweetheart, it's no big deal," Sidney said turning back over and puffing up his pillow.

"Sid?"

"Alright," he said turning the lamp on by his side of the bed and sitting up. "One of the things I love about you, and also scares me about you, is how impulsive you can be. It's alright when it is small things like growing mirlitons, whoever heard of mirlitons anyway, but bigger scarier things like going to a stranger's farm in the Barataria Basin to see his *mirliton trellis*, well you should have waited and let me go with you. That's out in the swamps, Leslie, no telling what kind of trouble you could have gotten into," Sidney told her.

"But it was okay and he wasn't an ax murderer. I am a pretty good judge of character and besides he is a gardener like myself," Leslie said.

"When we went to the farmers market and you bought some of those mirlitons, I thought you were crazy. Then when this farmer told you to come to look at how he grew them, knowing how impulsive you can be I offered to go with you.

The Cookbook

But no, on an impulse you went alone," Sidney said with fear in his voice. "Like you couldn't wait for me to go with you."

"I'm sorry, Sid, so this is about me going alone…"

"On an impulse…"

"Alright on an impulse…without you,"

"Yes, and Leslie you do this all the time. Since you have been writing cookbooks, I never know what you will do next. It was bad enough when we were working on criminal cases together and you would go off without letting anyone know what you were up to, but now I don't even know what leads you to go off on an impulse," Sidney told her. "If something were to happen to you, I wouldn't have the slightest idea of where to start looking. I know that sounds silly but, Les, we have worked enough cases together in my detective business for you to know that things happen, unexpected things."

"Okay. I promise to let you know when I have an impulse to do something impulsive. I love you Sid and I don't want to worry you. It's not good for your health and honey, forgive me, I just wasn't thinking," she said leaning over to hug him then puffing up her pillow laying back down. "Goodnight, sweetheart, I'm glad we talked about this. See you in the morning."

Sidney, still sitting up, looked over at Leslie and shaking his head in disbelief, sighed, then turning out the light he laid back down. Now wide awake, he stared into the darkness. Knowing sleep wouldn't come any time soon, he took a deep breath and began to pray for peace and rest.

Chapter 3

Once again Ryan sat in the courtroom listening to the Parole Board tell his grandfather, Nick, his Parole was denied. Nick turned around and looked at his grandson. Their eyes locked. Ryan sat stunned. *I thought surely this time they would let him out. What does it take?* he said to himself.

Nick had served five years of the ten for larceny. Now soon to be in his seventies, he wanted to get out so he could spend time with his grandson. They kept in touch through letters and occasional visits and phone calls. Nick had all the pictures and letters from Ryan and school pictures hung in his cell on the wall. Nick didn't hear from his daughter, Leslie, and he understood that but was grateful that his grandson had kept their line of communication open.

"Mom, I'm going to the parole hearing tomorrow if you would like to go with me," Ryan had asked his mother while they worked in her garden.

Once again she made some excuse not to go. Ryan accepted the relationship between his mother and grandfather although he didn't completely understand it. Nick never said much about it even when Ryan would share with him things Leslie was doing, like the cookbooks and her garden. Her explanation was always that she didn't know he existed until a few years ago and she didn't know him. However, she always encouraged Ryan's relationship with his grandfather.

During the time Nick awaited his trial, which took three years, Ryan and Nick spent quality time together. It broke Ryan's heart when they took him from the courtroom in handcuffs. Sitting next to his mother and father, he began to cry and call out to Nick. As a little eight-year-old boy, he only knew that they would be apart for a long time. He had no idea how hard it would be as he prayed for his grandfather's parole every day.

"Come on Ryan, there is nothing we can do," Annabelle told him.

They rose from their chairs as Nick left the room. This time he didn't even look back at Ryan. He held his head up high and left the courtroom through a door beside the table where the parole board had handed down there decision.

"Thank you, Annabelle, for coming with me. I appreciate it. Can I buy you lunch? I don't have to be back in class until two," Ryan said holding the outside door open for Annabelle.

"You're disappointed again that your mother didn't come with you today," Annabelle said across the table.

"I guess I am, but I really don't expect her to come with me although I invite her every time," Ryan answered.

"Someday you will understand your mother's position on the subject of your grandfather. She would never want to hurt you where this is concerned, Ryan, but she harbors a lot of hurt about your grandfather," Annabelle told him trying to help him deal with his emotions.

"I hope the day will come when we can talk about it," Ryan shared with Annabelle as they left the café. "Thanks again for coming with me."

*****

Leslie always had an uneasy feeling knowing Ryan was once again going to the Parole hearing for Nick. For Ryan's sake, it would be good if Nick was released. But she had to admit it would not be a good day for her. Many times she rehearsed what she would tell Ryan about his grandfather that kept her at a distance. There was no easy way to explain her reservations even though she had forgiven Nick for his transgression concerning her mother, Ryan's grandmother that he never knew, she still found it hard to forget.

She was glad that Annabelle went with Ryan to the hearing. As she waited to hear the outcome, she was preparing herself for the Board's decision when the phone rang.

"Hello," she said putting the cell phone on speaker.

"It's over and they aren't going to release him," Annabelle said from the Ladies room in the courthouse. "Ryan and I are going to that little café around the corner from the courthouse for lunch."

"Thank you for going with him," Leslie said feeling a little guilty.

"No problem. I'll call you later."

Chapter 4

The discovery of mirlitons at the farmers' market put Leslie on a new path of investigation. As a writer, she would do research to make sure the people and places were real for the readers. However, she now was researching a vegetable or some may consider it a fruit, and it was as intriguing to find its origins as it would be to run background checks on people.

Her trip to the farm where Ben, the farmer, showed her how to grow mirlitons put her in tune with her own organic garden. She placed the bulbs he gave her exactly as he instructed with the stem end covered in soil. Standing up, there was a sense of accomplishment as she looked out over her garden. *Father, thank you for all of your provisions. We plant our food in the soil you provide then wait for your sunshine and rain to help the plants grow. Then we nourish our body with the bounty. We are blessed, Lord. Help me to provide not only food for the body but food for the soul through these cookbooks. I ask in Jesus' Name. Amen.*

Molly Owen

She thought about what Sidney told her about being impulsive and wondered if he was concerned about something else. He had always trusted her instincts before, even relying on them to solve a case. Maybe his instincts had kicked in. Was he involved in a case that made him concerned about this farmer, Ben? Or was he just being overprotective of her? Either way, it was unnerving. Taking her work gloves off, she picked up her knee pad and put her tools in the basket and carried them to the garden shed, Sidney had built for her.

Back in her studio, she sat down at her desk and out of habit began to do a background check on Benjamin Buck. She discovered that he was a native of Barataria, south of New Orleans with his family going back several generations. He inherited his farm from his father. He had two siblings, a sister Mary and a brother Samuel. Nothing stood out in his history that was alarming and Leslie decided to let it go and get ready for the food stylist she had hired to make her recipes look appealing for the photographs in the cookbook.

She had set up a place in her studio for the photoshoots. Her recipes created in her own kitchen would be brought out to the studio where with the help of Pearl, a well-known food stylist in the New Orleans culinary world, would make a suitable plated display then spray with the secret spray that gave it that *just-out-of-the-oven* shine, where you could imagine the heat rising from the succulent ingredients. Leslie was always delighted with the outcome and envious of Pearl's talent. Then, Leslie, with her photography skills, would snap endless shots for later review. This was the process with each new exposure to a recipe. She prided herself in the background stories she included, with either the origin of the recipe or the unusual ingredient within the recipe that made it unique.

"Well, Miss Leslie, tell me more about these mirlitons you have planted," Pearl said with her dark blue eyes flashing.

"Surely as a New Orleans native, you have heard of mirlitons or Jerusalem artichokes as some are called," Leslie said putting the lens and filters back in the camera case.

"I have. But can't say I've eaten any of them," Pearl said with skepticism. "My momma is from Nova Scotia and she never heard of mirlitons and she is an excellent cook."

"Chayote is another name for them, maybe she has heard them called by that name. They're like squash and mostly used the same way but with a very different taste."

"You mean like stuffed chayotes?" Pearl said surprised.

"Yes, does your mother prepare them that way?" Leslie asked with enthusiasm.

"She does. You want me to ask for her recipe?"

"That would be great and I'll give her credit in the cookbook."

That night while eating dinner, including the latest new recipe from Leslie's kitchen, Sidney asked her about Nick's hearing. "No release," she said then obviously changing the subject, she told Sidney about her conversation with Pearl earlier that day.

Knowing not to push any further conversation on the subject of Nick he shifted to Leslie's observations about her conversation with Pearl.

"So, do you think we have had these, what are they called again?"

"Mirlitons."

"Yeah, mirlitons, but didn't know what they were?"

"I'm sure we have. Ben sells them to the restaurants in the Quarter and some of the upscale restaurants in uptown New Orleans."

"He does now? So is that your next step? Going into business with Ben selling produce?"

"What? Sidney, what is going on? Is there something I need to know? Why have you been acting so strange about this?"

"Oh. Don't mind me. I guess I'm just a little jealous. He is a fine-looking guy, seems healthy and all. By the way, is he married?"

"What are you saying?"

Sidney got up from the table and started to clear the dirty dishes. Leslie watched him take them to the kitchen. With his back to her, she saw him lower his head in prayer. Coming back to the table, he sat down and told her he had gone to the doctor without telling her and the report wasn't what he had hoped for.

Leslie reached across the table and took his hand.

"He wants me to cut back even more on my hours at work and it's possible I'll need by-pass surgery in the future," Sidney said.

"We're so blessed, Sid, to have a strong relationship with God. When I think of us trying to handle everything on our own without him, it scares me. We were very fortunate that you survived your heart attack and, Sid, whatever the future holds, with God by our side, we'll be alright. We must remember, it's God's will not ours."

"You are right, Les, and with your help, we will face this together. I love you," he said.

The Cookbook

"I love you too. So what are you going to do about work?"

"I thought we could cut back on our caseload and do more domestic investigations and less criminal. Charles could do the leg work and you and I could do more of the grunt work on the computer and phone. I could even do some of it from here because until we know how this will work, we may need to give up the office and work out of home or get a smaller office to save money. What do you think?" Sidney said waiting for her reaction to him being underfoot on a daily basis.

"Well, the first thing we need to do is get God involved and I can see it working from here. We rattle around in this big house anyway. We can rearrange your office to accommodate more filing cabinets. Its location in the house is perfect for clients if they need to come to your office. If you give up the building we can find a place here for Charles to hang his hat. I think it will work. Don't you?" Leslie said with confidence.

"You amaze me, Mrs. Rye. So we just shift gears, so to speak and *viola* we change everything and you're okay with it," Sidney said smiling at her.

"And, Sid, don't get it in your head for one minute that my studio is up for grabs," she said with a grin on her face and arms folded across her chest, "that is one line you can't cross."

"Understood," he said smiling at her.

"So when are you going to talk to Charles? You want to do it alone or do you want to invite him to dinner or how do you want to handle it?"

"Give us a few days, honey, to work things out. Then we can tell him together."

"I love you, Sid, it will all work out, you'll see and as far as the farmer Ben is concerned, you have nothing to worry about,

Sidney Rye, because you are stuck with me," Leslie said kissing his cheek. "Forever, remember?"

"I remember," he said remembering his blushing bride and the day they took their vows.

Chapter **5**

The sun shone brightly that Sunday as people gathered for prayer meeting at the Ryes. Even though the meeting was traditional in presentation with old familiar hymns and scripture readings, Ryan was bringing friends from college to the meetings and with them came some of the contemporary Christian songs the young people listened to.

At breakout time Ryan's group would retire to the upstairs den where they would study the Bible and sing. Their voices would fill the house and others would listen to the words of the songs. The type of music, for the most part, was unfamiliar but the words were powerful.

"Mom, may we please go with Ryan's group today?" the twins pleaded with hands together in prayer fashion under their chins.

"Check with your father," Annabelle told them while pouring a cup of coffee in preparation for the study part of their service.

"He said yes," the girls shouted as they ran giggling up the stairs.

"I hope Ryan is ready for this," Annabelle said to Leslie.

"Oh, I think he can handle it. He has a way with kids. He'll probably live up to the challenge," Leslie laughed as they went back to the living room.

"The problem is, our girls don't think they are kids any longer. They are so anxious to be grown-ups, it scares me."

"Yes, I remember that stage well," Leslie laughed again at her friend's concerns. "Say can we have lunch sometime next week?"

"Sure. Something going on we need to talk about?"

"A couple of things," she answered knowing that Annabelle could read her like a book.

Soon the groups gathered back together to share the pot luck meal. Some of the young people went outside with their plates and sat on the steps leading to the Galley. The conversation went to the lesson in their group study.

Ryan was pleased that a new person had come to the meeting. She was reserved, not shy, but in deep concentration during the scripture reading. He noticed how sweet she was in an unpretentious kind of way. Not a lot of makeup and dressed conservatively but yet confident in her appearance.

"So Karlah what did you get out of the study today?" Ryan asked noticing she seemed preoccupied.

"I was just thinking about that," she said, aware that the rest of the group was well versed in scripture. She felt a little uneasy afraid of saying the wrong thing.

"What is it that stood out to you?" he asked again.

"I guess it was how busy I am, with school, work, and volunteering and maybe I should take more time with God, studying His Word. I just don't know how to fit it into my schedule. You know what I mean?" she said confused.

"I know exactly what you mean. How do the rest of you feel about the question of making time to be with God?" he asked.

Each person in the group began to talk about their own commitments and their need to make more time for God's Word. They agreed that Sunday seemed to be the only time they really thought about it and maybe that was the concern they all had. Ryan asked if they had any suggestions to help with this concern. The twins both chimed in with the way their family dealt with this.

"We have a devotional after breakfast in the morning to start our day. We read the scripture then we talk about it," Amy said.

Followed by Jamie's statement. "It's just what we do. It's like taking time to be with a friend."

"It is an excellent way to start your day, in the Word, and it helps you during the day with relationships and decisions. My family did that and when I left for college, I continued. Sometimes I will sleep late or be late for class and I don't take the time to be with God. But, when I don't take the time I notice it because my day seems to go in every which direction and I feel unglued." Ryan told them.

"My mother says when she works in her garden she spends time with the Lord. So you can spend time with God anytime anywhere. So let's pray about it before we leave," Ryan said nodding to Karlah to start the prayer. *"Our Father, we come before you with a commitment to spend more time in your presence,"* she began.

"We desire to be in your Word and ask your help in this commitment. Knowing you lead us to a better understanding of who we should be in your sight, Lord, our prayer is for more of you in our daily life," Ryan continued.

"Thank you father, for loving us and watching over us," Jamie added.

"In Jesus' Name. Amen," Ryan said.

As the group began to break up, taking their plates back in the house, Ryan made a point to walk in with Karlah. He sensed a deeper concern than she had shared and was hoping she could share privately.

"Karlah, why don't you and I have coffee together sometime? I would like to get to know you better if you think we can find time in our busy schedules. My schedule is pretty tight with classes and all but if we really work at it, I think we could find the time. What do you say, can we do it?" he said with a grin.

"I think we can work it out, I would like that," she said to Ryan's delight.

Ryan hadn't had much time for dating since being at Tulane. It didn't mean he didn't want to date but finding the time between classes and study was more than he could handle. He hoped that he wouldn't disappoint Karlah by not finding a moment he could spend with her. He was sure she needed to

The Cookbook

talk about whatever was keeping her attention. If his homework schedule had not been so demanding he would have asked her out for coffee after their Sunday meeting and now he wished he had done just that since he was having a hard time finding time to meet with her on his calendar.

Later that week as he ran across campus he noticed Karlah walking in the same direction. He stopped in front of her and walking backward asked her how she was doing.

"Okay, I guess. Are you late for class?" she asked noticing his steps.

"Yes. But we still need to have that cup of coffee. I'll call you later," he said turning around. Then stopping he said. "How about Saturday morning?"

"That works for me. Where?"

"At my parents' house," he said. "Nine o'clock."

"Okay," she shouted as he took off running. She was encouraged by his effort to meet with her. It did not go unnoticed that he was handsome like his father.

Chapter **6**

Sidney brought out a basket of tools while Leslie grabbed some bulbs yet to be planted. It was a beautiful Saturday morning with the sun shining brightly requiring them to wear sunglasses. However, a storm was brewing offshore and was scheduled to arrive early next week so Leslie wanted to finish planting all the bulbs and seeds. It might end up being a gully washer and she wanted the plants to have enough time to get established before the rains came.

"So where do we begin? Do you want me to get more newspapers to put between the rows after I pull some weeds?" Sidney asked looking down the perfect rows with little sprouts popping up their little heads.

"Yes. That's a good idea, I think there is some newsprint in the shed," Leslie said putting on her gloves and laying the knee pad on the ground. "I think Ryan is meeting Karlah here around nine, so we can get a head start."

"Are they a 'thing'?" Sidney asked setting the papers down.

"I don't think so. It sounded like they were going to study together. I don't think either one of them has time for dating," Leslie shared.

"Do you know anything about Karlah, where she came from? I don't recall seeing her before, do you?" Sidney inquired not letting Leslie know his real reason for asking, keeping Jeffrey's promise to not let her and Annabelle know he was checking into things concerning Karlah.

"No. She just showed up on Sunday. But, I think it could have been an invitation from the Bordeaux twins because she is their gymnastics instructor. She is a student at Tulane, I think she is a freshman. I don't know if Ryan knew her before Sunday, but I doubt it. Why do you ask?" Leslie said.

"No particular reason. Just curious. Since our son is involved it would be nice to know more about her. Don't you think?" Sidney said.

"I guess so. I'm sure we will know more soon enough. I hear a car. That might be her now," Leslie said getting up to greet Karlah.

Just then Ryan drove in and parked next to Karlah's car. He got out of his truck and went around to greet her and show the way to Leslie's garden in the side yard. As they walked up to Ryan's parents, Leslie and Sidney stood up to meet them.

"Hi Karlah, it's good to see you again. Welcome to our garden," Leslie said.

"Actually it's Mom's garden. We're just helpers. But we do reap the harvest and that makes all the work worth it. Right, Dad?" Ryan said looking over at Sidney as he nodded his head in agreement.

The Cookbook

"Ryan told me that you are an author, and you are now writing cookbooks," Karlah said.

"That's true. I've written many fictional books mostly romance and mystery but I decided to branch out and write some cookbooks," Leslie told her.

"I would love to read some of your books. Maybe not in this season of my life, what with school and working, I don't have much leisure time," she said turning to Ryan for confirmation.

"Speaking of which, Karlah and I want to spend some time getting to know each other and thought we could do that helping you with the garden," Ryan said smiling.

"Great. Karlah have you ever worked in a garden before?" Sidney asked.

Karlah confessed she didn't know the first thing about gardening. She had never even had a houseplant to care for and was concerned that she may not be much help. But Ryan began to show her the ins and outs of organic gardening. He handed her a pair of gloves and a pad for her to kneel on and led her to the end of the garden where they would work pulling weeds and preparing the soil for planting.

"So what brought you to Tulane?" Ryan asked as he pulled a weed up by its roots.

"Well, I couldn't go on my own financially because…I'm basically on my own. So. I applied to several Universities for scholarships and/or work-study help and Tulane came through with a package deal and here I am."

"So you are not a native of New Orleans?" Ryan quizzed.

"Oh, yes, I was raised here, but my parents are deceased."

"I'm sorry Karlah, so how long have you been on your own?"

"I never knew my father, my mother told me he died before I was born and my mother died two years ago," Karlah said trying to pull a weed with a stubborn root system.

"Here, this tool will help. Just push it down beside the weed and dig it out," Ryan said handing her a fork looking tool.

"Any way that is why I'm at Tulane and why I work at the gym," she explained.

Overhearing their conversation, Sidney wanted more information and asked Karlah.

"Did your mother go to Tulane? I ask because perhaps that would also be a source of financial help." Sidney said.

"No. She didn't go to college. She was a single mother and had to work to support us. She had me two years out of high school. My father was killed in a job-related accident when she was pregnant."

"So, you are really alone in this world? I admire you for wanting to continue your education," Ryan said.

"My mother and I lived in the French Quarter in the back of a gym where she worked. She taught gymnastics. She was a hard worker right up until she got sick. She had cancer and the owners of the building where we lived let us stay there even when she couldn't work anymore. I was a senior in high school, so I worked part-time in the gym to help with the rent, went to school and took care of her," Karlah said with a catch in her voice.

"Is that where you live now?" Sidney asked.

"No, I live in the dorm at school,"

The Cookbook

"Well, the Bordeaux girls really enjoy having you as their teacher. They talk about you all the time," Leslie said trying to lighten things up, seeing how talking about her mother was emotional for her. "We are glad you came on Sunday. I suspect the girls were instrumental in that."

"Yes, they are really sweet, and I've been wanting to get back to church. So, it worked out great. I really enjoyed your message, Mr. Rye."

"Thank you, Karlah, you may call me Sidney,"

"And please call me Leslie. So you learned gymnastics from your mother," Leslie said thinking about her own mother. Raised by a single mother herself, she understood the deep bond Karlah had with her mother.

"Yes. She could have gone to the Olympics, that's how good she was,"

"Really, I bet you were really proud of her," Ryan remarked as he moved further down the row of plants.

"Yes, I miss her," she said.

"Any other family around here?" Sidney asked trying to get a handle on her life.

After a while, Leslie put a stop to all the questions as she noticed it was making Karlah uncomfortable. So with a 'no' answer to having any family close by, they moved on to talk more about themselves. Soon, Leslie asked Ryan and Karlah to stay for an early lunch and they agreed since both had studies to do and needed to get back to the campus.

All and all it was a pleasant visit and Ryan felt he understood more of what Karlah was dealing with and why she was open to learning more about scripture and how to make room for God in her busy life.

After lunch, Karlah helped Leslie clean up and then thanking her she told them she really needed to get going so she could study for exams on Monday.

"We have enjoyed getting to know you Karlah and hope to see you again soon, maybe in the morning at the prayer meeting," Leslie said giving her a hug.

"Yes. I'll be there," she said waving goodbye.

Chapter 7

Leslie waited in a booth at their favorite restaurant sipping on the sweet tea through a straw. Her thoughts mulling around in her mind. She wasn't sure how much to share about Sidney's health but she really needed to share. It had been heavy on her mind ever since Sidney told her about the doctor's appointment.

For the most part, Leslie dealt with Sidney's heart condition with strength and hope. She tried not to dwell on it and stayed busy to occupy her mind with other things, but lately, thoughts of him having another heart attack had set up residence in her mind and maybe if she shared her thoughts with Annabelle it would release some of her concerns.

Annabelle arrived and after scanning the room she located Leslie. She walked to the table as heads turned admiring her stark beauty when she passed. Leslie stood up smiling as she watched her friend in all of her finery come to her. The two women hugged each other lingering a little longer than usual.

Leslie found herself tearing up with emotion. As they sat down Annabelle asked Leslie what was going on.

"Is Sidney okay," she asked.

"Yes and no," Leslie said wiping her eyes with a napkin.

"What do you mean?"

"Oh, Annabelle, he hasn't been himself lately. Not unlike when he had that heart attack five years ago," she told her about his assumptions where Ben was concerned.

"He didn't really think you were attracted to this guy, did he?"

"I think it was more that, in his mind, Ben is healthy and maybe I would be better off with someone that didn't have health problems. I don't know what he was thinking. I just know it was upsetting," Leslie said dabbing at her eyes. "He went to the doctor without telling me so he must suspect something is going on with his heart."

Just then a cute young girl with pad and pencil in hand, smiling, walked up to the table to take their order. Noticing that Leslie was upset, the waitress told them she would give them a little more time to decide and she walked away. Annabelle put her wide-brimmed hat and white gloves in the chair beside her. At the jester, Leslie began to shake her head.

"What?" Annabelle, noticing her friend's reaction, said.

"You never change and believe it or not I take great comfort in that," Leslie said getting her emotions under control.

"So, let's see what we are in the mood for," Annabelle said raising the menu from the table.

The Cookbook

Leslie took her readers out of her purse and began to examine the menu. "I'm not very hungry so I'll just have a shrimp salad," she said laying the menu back on the table.

"I think I'll have a bowl of gumbo and a glass of sweet tea," she told the girl when she returned and Leslie put her order in for shrimp salad.

They took each other's hands and bowed their heads in prayer.

"Father, we thank you for this friendship, we are so grateful for your grace that surrounds us always. We love you, God, please give Leslie and Sidney strength and courage. Bless this food for our bodies. In Jesus' Name. Amen," Annabelle prayed.

They gave a little squeeze before letting go of their hands and Leslie echoed, *"Amen."*

"Okay, tell me more about Sidney's visit to the doctor."

"He told Sidney to slow down or he may need by-pass surgery sooner than later," Leslie said sipping on her glass of tea.

"What does that mean?" Annabelle asked, concerned.

Leslie told her of the plan to cut back on any criminal investigations which would affect Annabelle since Sidney's detective service did a lot of work for her. Then she said Sidney would move his business home so she could help him. Charles would do all the leg work and possibly move to their home also.

"Anyway it would be a major change but it would take a lot of pressure off Sidney," Leslie told her.

"How do you feel about this?"

"At first I told him my studio was off-limits. Teasing of course. But now it would make sense for him to set up in the studio and I could set up in his office which would be closer to the kitchen."

"It's worked very well having Jeffrey work in the quarters across the courtyard from our house. I think it would give Sidney his own space being in the studio."

"And I could still help and Charles would feel more comfortable. Thank you, Annabelle. I needed to talk to you and it is nice to run these ideas by you before approaching Sidney with them," Leslie said.

Then their conversation turned to Karlah and Leslie told Annabelle about when Ryan and Karlah came to the house and helped with the garden.

"They stayed for lunch. Sidney asked a lot of questions. I guess that is the investigator in him but Karlah opened up about her family," Leslie said.

"We really don't know much about her. The girls like her and she's a good instructor. I like the fact that safety comes first with all her students. I really don't see how she keeps up with everything with working and classes. Do you think she and Ryan are going to date?"

"I doubt it, they both are very busy. I think, after the Sunday when she came to our meeting, Ryan sensed a need for her to talk to someone about God." Leslie told Annabelle.

"I was pleased when she accepted the girl's invitation to come to our prayer meeting," Annabelle commented.

"She told us both her parents have passed. In fact, she didn't know her father. He died before she was born. She grew up in

The Cookbook

the French Quarter living with her mother behind that same building where she teaches now."

"Really, that's interesting. So she had a built-in clientele."

"Yes, her mother taught gymnastics until she got cancer and died two years ago. Even though she is a freshman, it took her awhile to be able to finance her classes. She is going on loans, scholarships, and work-study. I really admire her ambition," Leslie said. "Hearing her story brought back thoughts of my mother. Single, raising a child by herself. There are a lot of similarities in our background. It made me think about telling Ryan the whole story of his grandmother. But, because of the strong relationship he has with his grandfather, I think it would be difficult for him to hear."

"I understand. I told Ryan that day after the parole board hearing that someday he would understand your feelings about his grandfather," Annabelle told her.

"I guess he wishes I would tell him the reason it's so hard for me to see his grandfather. I did tell him long ago that for most of my life I didn't know Nick. So it's hard for me to think of him as my father," she said.

After lunch they walked out to flag down a taxi, each going their separate ways. The air hung down like a wet rag as they waited on the sidewalk. Annabelle fanned herself with some papers she held. Her white suit hugged her body as sweat trickled down her back.

"This humidity is awful today," she said.

"Here comes a taxi, you take it. I'll wait for the next one," Leslie said giving Annabelle a hug before telling her good-bye as she got into the taxi waving at Leslie as it drove off.

"Thank you, Father, for my friend Annabelle," Leslie said.

Chapter **8**

Sitting across the desk from Sidney, Charles asked. "How on earth did you talk Leslie into giving you her studio?"

"Actually it was her idea. She convinced me that it just made sense and she likes being set up in my office in the house because it's closer to the kitchen. So, everything has worked out for the best. Don't you think?"

"You won't get any argument from me. I think this is a perfect set up for us and our clients and our office fits nicely in this space. Does Leslie have enough space for what she's doing with her cookbooks?"

"She says she does especially with all of my things out of there," Sidney reassured Charles. "So now all we have to do is to let our clients know where we are and start weeding out some of the criminal cases. Not all of them but in the future, we will go more toward domestic work."

Molly Owen

"What are we doing about the case that Jeffrey wanted us to look into?" Charles questioned.

"I ran a background on the guy and came up blank. He and his present wife have one daughter that is in Karlah's Gymnastics class. All and all I didn't come up with anything unusual," Sidney told him.

"Perhaps Jeffrey should get to know this guy better. If they become friends, then this guy might open up," Charles said.

"Not a bad idea, the class, and parents are going out of town soon for competition in Houston. That would be a good time to build some relationships. I'll talk to Jeffrey about it and see what he says. This may not lead to anything. It could just be an over-cautiousness on Karlah's part. She lives in the dorms at the university so it's not like she lives alone."

"Knock, knock," Leslie said coming through the door to the studio. "Looks like you have set up shop. How's it working for you?"

They both assured her they were doing well and liked the space. She set a plate of muffins on the desk, hot from the oven.

"Wow, now this is a fringe benefit. We get to be the tasters for her kitchen products," Charles said taking a muffin.

"Don't ask what's in it or it will spoil the surprise," Sidney warned.

"I don't care what's in it. This is delicious, Lesley,"

"Thank you, Charles, and don't pay any attention to him," she said laughing as she went out the door and back to her kitchen.

Back in her kitchen, she set aside some of her muffins for Ryan to take back to the dorm after he had supper with them

The Cookbook

later that evening. She was looking forward to having a meal with him and was anxious for him to see the studio now that Sidney was settled in. She planned to surprise her men with a new recipe she was developing using the mirlitons from her garden.

Ryan was a little surprised that his dad and Charles were giving up their office on Canal Street but was glad Sidney would be close at home so Leslie could keep an eye on him. Although he was concerned after Sidney told him the doctor wanted him to cut back on his workload, he was confident that his dad would follow orders, especially with his mom close by.

"So, what do you think?" Leslie said dabbing her mouth with a napkin.

"About what?" Sidney teased knowing full well what she was referring too.

"The stuffed mirlitons," she answered a little frustrated.

"It was really good, mom," Ryan said putting the last bite in his mouth.

"The mirlitons are right out of our garden," Leslie said watching for their reaction.

"It is a lot like when you stuff zucchini, I like this different flavor. It's more Creole. Is that because of the seasoning?" Sidney asked.

"Yes. Pearl's mother gave me her version and it is more Cajun in flavor so I thought I would try this version to give the readers a choice," she said getting up and stacking the plates to clear the table. "Some Cajuns call the mirlitons chayotes."

"Not to change the subject, but isn't the Bordeaux family going to Houston soon for that Gymnastic competition?" Sidney asked.

"Yes, I think so. Why?"

"Just thought we should keep them in prayer. It is their first experience going out of town with the twins in competition," Sidney remarked.

"Your right, I better give Annabelle a call so I can give her some encouragement. Ryan, how does Karlah keep up with her studies and participate in this competition?"

"I really haven't talked to her lately. We are both busy and our schedules don't leave us much time to talk except on Sunday after meeting."

On the one hand, Lesley was glad to hear that they didn't spend time together. She thought it wasn't the right time for a serious relationship. However, she had the same feeling that Ryan had about Karlah's need to talk to someone. Maybe she should make the effort to talk to her, she thought. Perhaps she just needs a mother figure in her life. Someone to share with and get advice from.

Chapter **9**

They were blessed with a beautiful day for travel from New Orleans to Houston. The twins were overwhelmed with excitement and some apprehension for their first Gymnastic Competition. Annabelle and Jeffrey looked at each other and smiled as the girls couldn't stop talking all the way there and all through lunch. This was probably the most important thing they had experienced to date in their young lives.

They pulled up to the hotel and Jeffrey let Annabelle and the girls out with their luggage, then went to the parking garage to park. On his return, he met Annabelle at the desk where they checked in with the girls, wide-eyed since this was the first time staying in a hotel.

"Hi, Amy, Jamie. Isn't this exciting?" Sarah said as they hugged each other and danced around.

Sarah's father started laughing then said to Jeffrey. "Can you believe this?"

"I know. You would think they were going to meet, what's his name? You know their idol."

"Jeffrey, this is my wife Jennifer," he said, ignoring the idol reference.

"Hello, pleased to meet you. This is my wife Annabelle," Jeffrey said putting his arm around Annabelle's waist. "And this is Sarah's father Harry."

"You have a darling daughter," Annabelle said. "Our girls really like Sarah."

"Yes, we hear about your twins all the time. It's Amy and Jamie this, and Amy and Jamie do this, and so on," Jennifer said.

"Well, we better go to our rooms and get settled in," Harry said taking the handle of one of the suitcases and motioning for his daughter to get her suitcase, as they walked to the elevators.

Jeffrey asked the girls if they would like to get a drink while he took their luggage to the room and the three of them went to the hotel restaurant. Jeffrey managed the luggage cart and got on the elevator. On the way to their room, he ran into Harry again. He wasn't sure what to make of Harry. His wife seemed pleasant enough, but he sensed a nervousness from Harry. Perhaps he was just tired from the trip, he thought.

Annabelle and the twins order their drinks as more students and parents started arriving. Then Karlah came in and seeing them in the restaurant she went to their table.

"Hi girls. Are you ready for this?"

"Oh yes. This is so fun. Sarah and her parents are here too," Jamie told her.

"Her mother too?"

The Cookbook

"Yes. Her name is Jennifer. She seems very nice. They have gone to their room to get settled. Jeffrey took our suitcase to our room and he's coming back. You're welcome to join us," Annabelle told her.

"Thank You," she said sitting down next to Jamie. "I got here early this morning, so I'm settled in. I had to go to the event location and make sure we were checked in," Karlah said a little surprised but grateful to hear both of Sarah's parents would be there.

Jeffrey soon returned and told the girls their room was next door to Sarah's which sent a flurry of excitement at the table. Karlah looked at Jeffrey and asked what floor they were on. He assured her, knowing she was concerned, that the two families were the only two in the group on their floor. Seeing the relief on her face, Jeffrey gave her a smile.

Later that evening the two families decided to have dinner together at Jeffrey's suggestion, hoping he could learn more about this little family. While waiting for their food to come Annabelle asked Jennifer if she worked since she hadn't seen her at the gym and Jennifer told her she was a Realtor. She told her that Harry had his own business as a stockbroker and was able to be more involved with Sarah's activities.

"I know what you mean. Jeffrey and I share with getting the girls where they need to go. I'm an attorney and many times I'm in court so Jeffrey takes over," Annabelle said.

"Are you THE Annabelle Robicheaux? I followed the Bordeaux trial. You were magnificent. Then you married a Bordeaux and that's why the girls' last name is Bordeaux," Jennifer continued.

55

"I'm surprised you remember all of that since it was many years ago," Annabelle remarked not quite sure how to assimilate the observation.

"I know, but it was the talk of the town at the time. I'm sorry that wasn't a nice thing to say. I just feel so privileged to meet you," Jennifer said a little embarrassed. "Surely you were aware of the reputation the Bordeaux family and your own, for that matter, had back then."

The girls had stopped their chatter and were listening to Sarah's mother go on about the Bordeaux family causing the twins to look at their father with questioning eyes. He smiled and looking at Harry, asked if they lived in the Garden District.

"Yes. Not too far from the old Bordeaux estate. We wanted to buy it at the time it went on the market but someone beat us to it. It's a beautiful nice old home with lots of character. Is that where you grew up?"

"As a matter of fact, it is. My Sister Katrina Louise is a Realtor and she bought the place from the bank when it went into foreclosure and we, her siblings, helped get it ready for sale. It holds a lot of memories for all of us because we all grew up there and two of my sisters were married there.

"Annabelle lived in the French Quarter and I lived uptown when we got married. We now live in Annabelle's home in the French Quarter. Where did you live when you two got married?" Jeffrey asked as the girls lost interest in the conversation and went back to their giggling.

"Well, Jennifer is my second wife and we both lived in the French Quarter. Now we live in the Garden District. However, my first wife and I lived in a small place south of New Orleans called Barataria in Jefferson Parish. We loved it there, lots of history, because of its 19th century base for pirates and smugglers like Jean Lafitte. We owned a travel business that she ran and after she died I sold the business and moved back to the French Quarter where I grew up," Harry said.

"If you don't mind me asking, how did your wife die?" Jeffrey asked curiously.

"I don't mind. It was nineteen years ago. She died in childbirth. She gave birth to a little girl but our daughter also died," Harry said.

Jeffrey told him he was sorry to hear that while noticing how it still affected him. Soon their food arrived and during the meal, there was small talk about their children. However, Jeffrey and Annabelle were both involved in thoughts related to their previous conversations.

Later after the girls were asleep Jeffrey asked Annabelle what she thought of the Burkes. Nodding her head in contemplation she shared her feelings after meeting Sarah's parents.

"Jennifer gave me an uneasy feeling when she talked about Jonathan's trial. It was like she knew our families the way she talked about the Bordeaux and Robicheaux family like she knew all about us. I don't know, don't you find it strange that she remembers all that happened during that time. I mean she knew details I had long forgotten. She also mentioned that she knows your sister, Katrina Louise," Annabelle told him.

"So how does she know Katrina Louise?"

"She made some reference to them both being Realtors like they were partners or something. As I said, she seemed to be trying to impress me. But I wasn't impressed," Annabelle said.

"I find it interesting that Jennifer is his second wife. He told me his first wife died in childbirth and so did the baby."

"Oh, that's sad. Did they live here in New Orleans?"

"No, they lived in a place called Barataria south of New Orleans," he told her.

"Yes. I know that place. My father would take me there. There's a lot of history there mostly about Jean Lafitte."

"That's the place. I'm surprised you and I didn't run into each other because that's where my folks took me for history lessons," Jeffrey said smiling.

"I don't like to judge her, but, Jennifer doesn't seem to be the motherly type. You know what I mean?" Annabelle asked.

"Yes, I got that impression, too. However, you should have seen Harry's face when he talked about the daughter he lost when his wife died. I felt sorry for him," Jeffrey told her. "And he seems proud of Sarah. So he's obviously the parent in her life. I guess one is better than none."

Later during the competition, Jeffrey observed Harry staring at Karlah more than once. One time Harry caught Jeffrey looking and immediately turned his stare away from where Karlah was standing. Jeffrey thought that was odd behavior for a devoted father. He wondered if Harry and Jennifer were having marital problems. Or did he just have a roving eye? Either way, he now understood Karlah's reservations and looked forward to relaying information to Sidney. He also wanted Sidney to run a background check on Jennifer.

*****

"So this is your new space," Jeffrey said looking around. "I like it, even better than your previous office space. How do you guys like it?"

The Cookbook

"It's compact but workable and more importantly affordable," Sidney told him. "How was your trip to Houston?"

"That's what I wanted to talk to you about," Jeffrey said pulling up a chair next to Charles and sitting across the desk from Sidney.

He began by telling them his reservations about Harry Burke and Annabelle's observation about his wife Jennifer. He also told them how he caught Harry staring at Karlah.

"But, then, this morning I got a call from Harry and he wants to have lunch today at a place I'm not at all familiar with. I got the idea that he doesn't want our meeting discovered," Jeffrey said leaning back in his chair with a puzzled look.

"Are you saying it appears that he wants to share something with you but wants to make sure nobody sees the two of you together?" Sidney asked.

"It sure looks that way. What I can't figure out is who are we hiding from?"

"His wife?" Charles asked.

"I thought about that too. But why me? Why does he want to confide in me?"

"Didn't you say he caught you seeing him staring at Karlah?"

"Yeah, maybe. I just find the whole thing kind of strange. Anyway, I'll let you know later. In the meantime could you check on Jennifer? She seemed infatuated with Jonathan's trial and went on about what a fascinating event it was and how she admired Annabelle's performance at the trial. Annabelle couldn't believe the things Jennifer remembered, after all, it was a long time ago," Jeffrey said getting up and shaking hands with Charles, then, Sidney as he walked him to the door.

*****

Annabelle sat at her desk looking out at the courtyard trying to motivate herself to get busy. She couldn't get her mind off the past few days with the girls in Houston. Shaking her head she reached for her cell phone and punched Leslie's number.

"Good morning, Annabelle," Leslie said answering her phone.

"It is a sunshiny morning isn't it?"

"What's up? You sound like the cat that swallowed the canary, as they say," Leslie commented knowing Annabelle's moods.

"I've been mulling over something that happened this weekend in Houston. You have heard the girls talk about Sarah? Well, her father Harry is the only one that ever brings her to the gym. In fact, none of us including Karlah even knew if there was a wife, mother in the picture. Well, there is, and her name is Jennifer and I must say she is a piece of work," Annabelle said with a big sigh.

"What do you mean?"

"She acted as if she knew me. She knew my maiden name was Robicheaux and that I was Jonathon's attorney at his trial and, Leslie, she remembered things I had long forgotten. She went on and on about it until it got the girls' attention especially when she started talking about the Bordeaux name and how now she knew where the girls got that name. It was very unnerving and quite embarrassing. There is something not right about the whole thing. Harry told Jeffrey his first wife and a baby girl died in childbirth, and Jennifer was his second wife. Have you ever been to Barataria?"

"Yes, as a matter of fact. That is where Ben, the farmer lives. You know the one I bought the mirlitons from at the market and then upset Sidney by going out there without him to see Ben and have him show me how to grow mirlitons. Why?" Leslie said, a little curious.

"Harry, Sarah's father, and his first wife lived there when she died. They owned and she ran a travel agency. After she died, Harry sold it and moved back to the French Quarter."

"Is that where he met Jennifer?"

"I don't know. Jeffrey said Harry got emotional when he told him about his first wife and choked up talking about his baby girl. Jeffrey felt sorry for him. And something else that was strange was the way Harry looked at Karlah," Annabelle said changing her tone of voice.

"What are you saying?"

"Not in a lustful way. I can't explain it. Almost in a prideful way. Like I said it's very strange indeed. No wonder Sidney was upset with you about going to Ben's farm. It's a long way out there and full of swampland. I wouldn't think of going out there alone."

"Well, don't worry I won't be going back with or without him. Not after the fuss, he made about it," Leslie assured her friend.

"Anyway, I'm glad we talked. Do you know how somethings just nags at you? Well, this was nagging at me, but now I've got it off my chest so I can let you go back to work and I need to get busy, too. I love you, Leslie, thanks for listening," Annabelle said before hanging up.

Leslie sat enveloped in the conversation she and Annabelle had just had. There were more questions she wanted answers to for some reason. Maybe she would do some digging when she had more time. For now, she had some writing to do.

The Cookbook

Chapter **10**

No cookbook from New Orleans could be written without a recipe for Southern Shrimp and Grits. So today she was determined to create the best shrimp and grits recipe ever eaten. Everything from fresh off the boat shrimp to the creamiest grits would be the secret to her recipe.

The shrimp came fresh from a reliable fishmonger at The Market in the French Quarter. She began by peeling the shrimp and removing the tails. By using a deveining tool she could carefully remove the veins, running the tool along the curve of the shrimp. She slathered the shrimp with melted butter and a special blend of spices and put them individually on parchment paper on a cookie sheet. While she kept an eye on the shrimp cooking in the oven, she began to prepare the grits by whisking in boiling water with butter and salt. Adding her secret combination of cheese and spices to the creamy grits, she spooned it into bowls. Taking the shrimp from the oven, she laid a few on top of each bowl of grits. She set two bowls on a tray and took them out to her tasters in the office in her backyard.

"Knock, knock," she said pushing the door open with her hips while balancing the tray in front of her.

"Wow, that smells yummy. What is it?"

"My version of shrimp and grits, southern style, topped with mascarpone cheese, I made myself. This is the same cheese I use when I make Tiramisu and other sweet desserts, but this time I made it with the same spices I used in the grits," she said putting one bowl each in front of Charles and Sidney.

"You are really spoiling us with all this food. But, we really don't mind, so keep it up," Charles said before taking a big bite that burnt his mouth.

"Sorry, it is really hot off the fire," she told them. "So what are you guys working on?"

"Several things," Sidney said giving Charles a 'don't say anything look.'

"Anything I can help with? I'm a pretty good researcher," she said.

"We don't have anything right now but we will keep that in mind," Sidney told her with a wink.

After she left, Sidney reminded Charles of the promise he made to Jeffrey to keep the girls out of Karlah's concern about Harry.

"Yeah, I remembered that just before I almost spilled the beans," Charles told Sidney rolling his eyes. "That is the tricky part about Leslie popping in unannounced. But, I'm not complaining because this is absolutely delicious," he continued putting the last bite in his mouth.

The Cookbook

"I thought about that. I really don't like keeping things from Leslie and she could be a big help. I guess I better talk to Jeffrey because if we are going to work this case we may need her help," Sidney said putting the empty bowl down. "Boy that was good, she is an excellent cook, writer, and researcher, not to mention a wonderful wife and mother."

"Yeah, you are a lucky man, Sidney," Charles said a little envious.

"Yes, I am," Sidney said silently thanking God for his good fortune.

Back in Leslie's kitchen, she was finishing cleaning up after her mess made by preparing the Shrimp and Grits dish. Anxious to hear Sid's and Charles' take on the dish, she was convinced it was a winner and was ready to have Pearl stylize it soon. However, she would wait and prepare it when Ryan was coming for dinner.

It had not gone unnoticed when Sidney gave Charles a 'don't say anything look' when she asked about the cases they were on. So she surmised that it was a case involving someone she knew. Later she would see if Sid would tell her and if not she would have to let it go. *Oh, Lesley, do stop with your curiosity. It will just get you into trouble.* She told herself, returning to her kitchen chores. *But, who could it be?* She asked herself again ignoring her self-scolding. Just then Sidney came into the kitchen with two dirty bowls and spoons and set them in the sink.

"You outdid yourself on this one. Is it going in your cookbook?"

"Yes. I think it's a winner, don't you?"

"Well, you have two votes, if they count, and that cheese was wonderful, I have a feeling it's probably not good for my heart though so next time you can leave it off my bowl," Sidney said giving her a hug and kissing her cheek.

"If you noticed, your bowl only had a dab, you should have seen Charles's bowl," Leslie assured him.

"See you after a while. I love you." Then turning around Sidney left through the back door before Leslie could ask him the question burning in her thoughts.

Chapter **11**

Early morning fog covered the Garden District all along St. Charles Avenue. Leslie loved it when the fog came in off the Gulf. It was romantic, alluring, and mysterious inspiring many of her books. It was times like this she longed to return to writing romance novels. Looking out the front door she imagined how, in earlier times, the dark side of New Orleans took place in a morning like this. The image of the above-ground graves in the cemetery full of rituals by voodoo believers came to mind.

Remembering what Annabelle had said about going to Ben's farm in the swamps of Barataria Basin alone brought to mind her conversation the previous night with Sidney about the case they were working on. She found it interesting that she and Annabelle had just had a mysterious conversation about the very thing Sidney and Charles were investigating.

"Leslie, we haven't put all the pieces together on this but Jeffrey is paying for it and I can't really tell you why. He doesn't want Annabelle to know he is doing this either," Sidney told her.

"What do you mean you can't tell me why," Leslie asked puzzled.

"Because it's confidential," he answered sternly with a look that told Lesley he was serious.

"Okay," she said, letting him know she understood.

Not quite sure the direction their investigation would take them, Sidney asked Leslie to do some research on the travel agency owned by Harry and his first wife. This may take some searching since that was all she had to go on. No name. Just Harry Burke's first wife and a travel agency located in Barataria twenty-some years ago.

Leslie began her search in public records starting with marriage licenses. After all, she did have Harry Burke's name. Now all she needed was the other name on the license. *There it is*...Patricia Swanson, she said out loud. *Now let's see what we can find out about Patricia Burke.* She found her birth date, parent's names, and date of her death. The death certificate stated cause as childbirth. Following up on that information she looked for the name of the baby. Finally, she found an obituary for Patricia Burke and Patsy Burke buried the same day. Patsy Burke was listed as the stillborn daughter of Harry and Patricia Burke. Reading the obituary her heart went out to Harry. What a shock that would have been.

When Sidney talked to Jeffrey about having Leslie do some research on Harry and his first wife, Jeffrey gave him permission but reminded him not to let Annabelle know anything just yet.

"How did the lunch with Harry go?" Sidney had asked.

Jeffrey's answer was very vague which puzzled Sidney but he didn't push because he knew when Jeffrey wanted to share the information he would.

The morning fog began to lift, revealing the surroundings. Soon the sun shone brightly through the window finding Leslie hard at work on the computer searching for all information about the Burke's and recording it so she could send it to Sidney. She found the information intriguing and kept having to set aside her desire to start another novel based on Burke's story that was unfolding. Before long she sat up stretching then taking a deep breath she closed her laptop, saved her work and headed to the kitchen.

Looking at the clock, she realized it was past time for lunch. Opening the refrigerator she stood, scanning the items, then pulled out a few things to make a salad. She turned around when Sidney came through the back door.

"I bet you're getting hungry," she said leaning over for a kiss.

"Yeah, I'm beyond hungry, I'm starving. I was hoping we could have a bowl of leftovers from last night. But, the salad will do," Sidney said teasing.

Putting the salad back in the refrigerator and getting the leftovers from the night before, she got out two plates and began to spoon the food onto them. Placing the plates, one at a time, in the microwave, she turned to Sidney and asked, "How are things going out there?"

"Okay, I think we got a lead on a case we are working on," Sidney said picking at the food on the plate waiting to go into the microwave.

Molly Owen

"Stop that, Sid, your plate is almost ready. Which case are you talking about?" Leslie said moving the plate away from him.

"The Harry Burke case. By the way, how are you coming on your research?"

"I've located his first wife, her name was Patricia and the baby girl's name was Patsy," Leslie told him taking the plate out of the microwave and handing it to him.

"Well, an interesting tidbit, Jennifer was in real estate and listed the travel agency when Harry put it up for sale," Sidney said heading for the table.

Soon Leslie's plate was ready and she joined him at the table. The room was silent as they began to eat. Then Leslie said looking out the window. "My feelings about Patricia and her baby are that she was very different from Harry's second wife. I wish you could let me in on more than you are telling me. There has to be more to this than even you know."

"My thoughts exactly. Jeffrey had kind of a rendezvous with Harry the other day for lunch. When I asked him about it, he declined to comment. Something about confidentiality. But he wasn't really clear either. So there may be more to this than any of us know. I have the feeling Jeffrey now knows something but is not at liberty to share. Which would account for him avoiding me."

"What? I haven't noticed him avoiding you. He didn't seem any different on Sunday at the prayer meeting. By the way, Karlah wasn't there Sunday. Did you ask Ryan about that?" Leslie said

"Why would I ask Ryan about Karlah? I don't think they are an item so why would he know anything about Karlah. He

The Cookbook

wouldn't know any more than we do, is what I'm saying," Sidney explained.

At that, Leslie dropped the subject. She could always tell when she and Sidney were not on the same page. Over the years she had learned to move on and not pursue it, causing a discord, no matter how frustrating it was not to be able to clarify the misunderstanding or draw a mutual conclusion. However, she was very curious about this rendezvous Jeffrey had with Harry and wondered how much Annabelle knew by now.

Chapter **12**

As usual, Ryan was running late for a lecture on the other side of the campus and, of course, it was raining for the third day in a row. Pulling his hood up around his face with one hand, and holding tight to his book and spiral inside his blazer with the other hand, he made his way toward the building where his class was held. When he barreled through the door he almost ran over Karlah who was preparing to come out of the building.

"Oh, sorry… Is that you Karlah?" he said, stopping to make sure she was alright.

"Yes, I'm okay. Late for class?" she said grinning.

"Always. Hey, a group of us are going to Elizabeth's, you know that diner over in Bywater where students hang out," he said

"Yeah, I've been there once or twice," Karlah said stepping aside to let another student pass.

"Why don't you come tonight? You probably know some of them from the Sunday meeting. It will be fun," he said.

"What time?"

"Oh, around 5:30 before the late supper crowd," he told her making his way down the hall away from her.

"Okay. See you there," she shouted over the students rushing for class.

After lost study time going to Houston for the gymnastics competition she hadn't done much outside of studying every chance she got. Going to Elizabeth's might just be the break she needed. Even though a couple of years older than most of the other freshmen, she enjoyed the company. So, after her last class, she headed to her dorm room. On her way across campus, she got a glimpse of someone standing in the rain outside her dorm building. At first, she didn't recognize who it was, but as she got closer it became apparent that it was Mr. Burke.

"Hello, Mr. Burke. What are you doing here in the rain?" she asked sternly.

"Looking for you. I didn't get a chance to tell you how proud I was of our daughter at the competition in Houston. You are doing a very good job teaching the students," he said coming up with a reason to be lurking outside her dorm.

"Mr. Burke, I don't believe you. Please stop following me or I will call the police, or better still I will tell your wife," Karlah said starting to shake.

"Karlah, I don't mean any harm. Please, I will go," he told her and turned to walk away.

To make sure he was going, she stood in the rain and watched him leave the campus. Finally, she went inside. Her

The Cookbook

roommate wasn't in the room when she got there. She picked up her phone and dialed Jeffrey's number.

"Karlah? Are you alright?" Jeffrey said seeing her name on his cell phone.

"I'm not sure. Mr. Burke was waiting outside my dorm just now, in the rain and when I confronted him and threatened to call the police he left," Karlah said with anger and fear in her voice.

"Did he give a reason for being there?"

"Yes, but it was obvious he came up with it on the spur of the moment. Something about how proud he was of the job I was doing and how proud he was that his daughter did so well at the competition in Houston,"

"Okay, Karlah, he is gone. So, just be on alert. I'm sure he doesn't mean any harm," Jeffrey said trying to reassure her.

"I told him to stop following me or I would call the police or tell his wife," Karlah said still angry and not sure why Mr. Bordeaux was not taking her seriously.

"I understand your concern and Karlah I have someone checking him out. Someone I trust. If he comes up with any reason for your alarm I will let you know immediately," Jeffrey told her hoping she wouldn't do anything rash.

Karlah began to calm down and thanked Jeffrey for checking into Mr. Burke. They hung up and she began to get out of her wet clothes and get dressed to go out. She was glad Ryan had invited her to join his friends for supper. She needed to be with people so she could get her mind off Mr. Burke.

"Hi Karlah, glad you could make it. Come on and let me introduce you to some people," Ryan said leading the way to a table surrounded by students. Some of them Karlah knew and the others Ryan introduced.

She sat down next to Ryan and looked at the menu. Still shaken by the earlier encounter with Mr. Burke she tried to relax. Soon, she was in conversation with the others at the table. Unaware that Ryan sensed something was wrong, she tried to fit in. After the food came, she excused herself to wash her hands.

In the restroom, she began to shake again. Splashing water on her face, helped her to calm down. *"Why me, what does he want?"* she asked herself, looking in the mirror. Remembering the conversation with the group at the Rye's she bowed her head in prayer, *"Father, Almighty, I ask for your protection. He is a husband and a father, please let him see the harm he might cause if he continues his actions. Help me to handle this situation with grace, strength, and kindness. God, I don't want any harm to come to Sarah or her parents. Please just make this go away. In Jesus' Name. Amen."*

When she came out of the restroom Ryan was waiting for her. "Are you okay? You don't seem yourself. Are you upset about something?"

"Let's eat our dinner and perhaps we can talk about it later," she said with a smile.

Ryan was satisfied with Karlah's suggestion that they talk later and he was prepared to listen to whatever was upsetting her. He thought perhaps he could help in some way. They finished their meal and Ryan suggested he get a ride from Karlah back to campus since he had come with a friend.

"Yes, I'll be glad to take you back. In fact, it will make me feel safer to have you with me," Karlah said.

They walked to her car and Ryan noticed she scanned the area around them as they went a couple of blocks to where she was parked. He opened her door to let her in, then went around to the passenger side and got in.

"This is a nice car," Ryan said.

"Thank you, it was my mother's," she told him

"I drive my grandfather's old pickup. I just can't seem to give it up. I keep thinking I'm saving it for him, but he may never be able to drive it again," Ryan told her.

"Why?"

"Well, it's a long story but he is in jail and his parole keeps getting denied. I'll tell you about it sometime but right now are you ready to tell me why you don't feel safe and why you were so upset earlier?"

Karlah began to tell Ryan, from beginning to present her experiences with Sarah's father. She told him about her conversation with Mr. Bordeaux and how he was checking things out concerning Mr. Burke. Then she told him what had happened earlier that day by her dorm.

"I agree, that doesn't make sense. What did Jeffrey…Mr. Bordeaux say when you told him," Ryan said a little confused.

"That's just it. He didn't seem concerned and told me he had someone checking Mr. Burke out and would let me know if there was anything to be concerned about," Karlah said pulling into a parking space in front of her dorm and turning off the engine and the lights. She looked at Ryan lowered her head and began to cry.

"I'm sorry Karlah, I know you must be really concerned about this. I'm not sure I understand. How long has Mr. Bordeaux known about this?"

"Several weeks. Before we all went to Houston. He told me he knew someone who could run a background check on him and would let me know what he found out," Karlah said wiping her face with the handkerchief Ryan gave her from his pocket.

"Karlah, I have an idea of who is doing the background check. I can't say anything right now but I promise you I will get to the bottom of this and get back to you with what I find out. And, Karlah, please don't hesitate to call me at any time. Here is my cell number," he said taking a pen from his pocket and writing it down on a piece of paper he found on the console between them.

"Thank you, Ryan. I prayed while I was in the restroom. Can you and I pray?"

"Yes," Ryan said taking her hand and bowing his head. *"Father, we come to you with concerns over the attention Mr. Burke is giving Karlah. We ask that you keep her safe and give her peace so she can handle this. We pray also for Sarah's father that he will realize what he is doing isn't right and will leave Karlah alone. Thank You. In Jesus' Name. Amen."*

After walking her to her dorm room, he walked back to his dorm all the while thinking about what Karlah had told him. The first thing he was going to do was talk to his dad. He was sure that's who Jeffrey was having to do a background check. Maybe his dad could shed some light on the situation. If his dad couldn't reveal what was going on he would talk to Jeffrey because he thought Karlah's fear was genuine and she needed some answers. If nothing else Jeffrey could talk to Sarah's father and put a stop to him following Karlah.

Chapter **13**

Satisfied with two finished recipes to add to her cookbook, Leslie was getting the studio prepared for, Pearl, the food stylist. While she waited for her she set up the camera, lighting and white screen that went behind the plates of food. Soon she heard a knock at the studio door and setting the camera down, she went to open the door letting Pearl inside.

"Hi Pearl, I'm really excited about this session. It is so fun to see these pictures. By the way, how is your mother? The last time you were here she didn't feel well," Leslie said.

"She's doing better. I told you she is pregnant," Pearl said.

"No. How old is she? I'm sorry it just worries me when I hear of older women having babies. So much can go wrong," Leslie said bringing out the plates of food. "How's this? Too much cheese?"

"I think that's fine, once I put the spray on it'll be alright. My mother had me when she was fifteen. She's still in her

Molly Owen

thirties," Pearl said as she arranged things in front of the screen then smoothing the white tablecloth under the plate she stood back and examined the display.

"That looks good, Pearl, and I'm sorry for prying. I'm happy for her and pray for an easy birth," Leslie said adjusting the angle before snapping the picture. "What hospital is she going to?"

"She's having a home birth as she did with me. She's having the same midwife. This will be my mother's fifth child, so she knows how it's done." Pearl said laughing.

"Wow, not me. I had Ryan at the hospital. Your mother's braver than I was," Leslie said moving a little closer then snapping the final picture.

"Well, I think that will do for this time. I have a job to do uptown at a chocolate store. They make their own chocolate and want me to stylize it for their catalog," Pearl said as Leslie walked her to the door.

"That's great, Pearl, I'm glad your business has taken off. I'll give you credit in my cookbook also and maybe that will get you some more business."

"Thank you I appreciate it," she said.

"Give my best to your mother. I'll say a prayer for her," Leslie said.

*****

That evening Ryan showed up unexpectedly for dinner. Since she had prepared for the photoshoot she had plenty of food. As soon as he got there, Ryan, went out to the Studio in back to see his dad. Charles had just left so they were alone.

The Cookbook

"Dad, I have something to ask you and I hope you can give me an honest answer," Ryan said sitting across from Sidney.

"What is it, son?"

"It's about Karlah," Ryan said waiting for a reaction.

"Go on," Sidney said trying not to react.

"Karlah has been having a situation that has really frightened her. She told me about it last night after an encounter with one of her student's father. When she returned to her dorm, in the rain, he was waiting for her. He's been following her and she got really angry and told him she would call the police or tell his wife if he didn't leave her alone. She was really upset, Dad, and she told me that Jeffrey was looking into it and had someone doing a background check on him. So, my question is, are you doing a background check for Jeffrey on this Mr. Burke?" Ryan said.

Looking at Ryan in silence, Sidney weighed the situation. He had an obligation to his client however his son had asked him a direct question and was expecting an honest answer. Getting up and walking around the other side of his desk he leans back against it with his hands behind him placed on the desk.

"The answer is not an easy one. You see I'm in a touchy situation here, son. Your question involves a matter of integrity. I don't make a habit of revealing information concerning my clients. Now, that said, since Karlah told you about Jeffrey's efforts to help her. I suggest you take it up with him," Sidney said.

"Karlah did call him and she felt like he wasn't concerned. So if he's supposedly helping her why did she have that feeling?"

"Ryan, I can't answer for someone else. You need to talk to Jeffrey. I suggest you do it very soon. We don't want Karlah worrying more than she needs to, do we?"

"No. But, Dad, she was crying she was so upset."

"Even more reason to talk to Jeffrey. And, Ryan, I prefer you not mention this to your mother, understood?"

"Yes sir, I'll talk to Jeffrey after supper," Ryan said yielding to his father's advice.

*****

Ryan thanked his mother for another great meal and not lingering any longer, said goodbye. He then headed straight for Jeffrey's home in the French Quarter. Parking about two blocks away he hurried down the sidewalk in front of where they lived.

The Bordeaux family foursome was having a jam session. Annabelle on the harp, Jeffrey on the piano, Amy was playing the flute and Jamie a clarinet. Ryan could hear the music from where he stood out front by the gate on the sidewalk. He dialed Jeffrey's cell number. He heard the music stop and Jeffrey answered the phone.

"Hello, Ryan what can I do for you?" he said leaving the room and going to the kitchen.

"My Dad said I needed to talk to you about Karlah and I'm outside your gate," he said. "Could you come down and maybe we can go across the street to the bakery if they are still open and have a cup of coffee."

"I'll be down in a minute," Jeffrey said. He turned to Annabelle and the girls and told them Ryan needed to talk to him.

"Is everything okay?" Annabelle said.

The Cookbook

"Yes. Just something about the university," he lied as not to raise any concerns.

On his way down to meet Ryan, he formulated in his mind how much to divulge to Ryan. The whole thing was getting sticky and he wasn't excited about being involved at this stage. He had forgotten, that Ryan knew Karlah and, for all he knew, they were dating. This was going to be uncomfortable, to say the least, so he would have to watch what he said.

"Hi Ryan," he said opening the gate. "I don't think the bakery is open this late. Why don't we go to my office," he offered to let Ryan come through the gate.

When they were inside Jeffrey turned on the lights and asked Ryan to sit down. "Now, what is it you want to talk to me about?"

Ryan told Jeffrey what had happened when Karlah went to her dorm and how frightened she was. And when she told him what had been going on, he figured out that his Dad must be doing the background on Mr. Burke, and when he confronted his dad about it, he told him to take his questions to Jeffrey.

"So, Karlah is really upset and thinks you're not concerned," Ryan said hoping for some clarification.

"I'm sorry I gave her that impression, Ryan, but believe me when I say if I thought she was in any kind of danger I would protect her. I have information that I cannot reveal to anyone, not even your father. But, be assured Karlah is safe. Nothing is going to happen to her. The best thing you can do for her is to reassure her and be supportive," Jeffrey said.

"How can I reassure her when I don't know what's going on?"

"Tell her you have talked to me and that you trust me. You do trust me, don't you?"

"Yes sir," Ryan told him.

"Then help her believe it too," Jeffrey instructed.

He walked Ryan down the walkway between the buildings back to the locked gate. Opening the gate he assured him once again that it would be alright.

"Thank you for talking to me Jeffrey, I do feel better about it knowing that you are aware of the situation."

"You're welcome. Take care of Karlah," Jeffrey said as he shut the gate behind Ryan.

Jeffrey took a deep breath and walked back to the house. He knew he would have to talk to Harry, the sooner the better, he thought. His next hurdle would be Annabelle. So far he had been able to keep her out of it. But, now he knew she would have to know as much as he was allowed to tell her. Keeping secrets was not something he enjoyed especially from his wife.

*****

"And how long have you known about this?" Annabelle said to Jeffrey.

The girls were in bed and this was their private time when they could relax with a glass of wine and share the happenings of their day. However, Jeffrey knew this time would be clouded by what he would tell Annabelle about Harry.

"Since before we all went to Houston," he said taking another sip of wine.

Annabelle wasn't sure how to react. Her first impulse was anger followed by disappointment in Jeffrey's lack of trust in her. She took a deep breath and then shared with him her own feelings about the thing he wasn't willing to share earlier.

The Cookbook

"I'm sorry you felt compelled to keep this from me. Even when it could involve our girls. Karlah's teacher, and what happens to her affects them. I'm assuming since Ryan came to you that Sidney is involved and possibly even Leslie which would put her in the position of not sharing with me either. Do you see what a wicked web you have woven by not sharing with me?" Annabelle said taking her feet out from her comfortable position next to him on the couch and putting them on the floor in front of her.

"You have every right to be upset with me. It is obvious I didn't think it through. It all began when Karlah shared her feelings with me about Harry and how she thought he was following her. I volunteered to have him checked out. Until that took place I wasn't going to get you or Leslie, for that matter, involved. When Sidney couldn't find anything in his background to warrant concern I was going to drop it," he confessed.

"And now he's waiting for her at her dorm in the rain. Don't you think that's concerning?"

"There's more to this, Annie, than I can share," he said.

"Really, so now, even though you have told me what's going on you are still holding back information?"

"Annie, please trust me," Jeffrey begged.

"I'm going to bed," she said, setting her glass of wine on the coffee table and walking out of the room.

This was the last straw. This was interfering with his marriage and he couldn't let that happen. First thing in the morning, he would talk to Harry.

Chapter *14*

The Market was buzzing with locals and visitors to this famous place in the French Quarter. Weekenders from outside New Orleans were shopping for the next week while others had just come to look. The Rye's were making their way to the veggies. Pushing their way through the crowd was proving to be a challenge.

Holding hands so as not to be separated, Leslie told Sidney that this would be the last time they came on a Saturday. Finally, they arrived at Ben's booth.

"Well, hello you two," he said as he sacked some vegetables and handed it to a customer.

"How's your business?" Sidney asked.

"Really good. I'm sold out of tomatoes and green onions," he told them.

"I see you still have mirlitons. I had an idea for you and me," Leslie said to Ben.

"Yeah, what's that?"

"Well, two things. Type up a recipe using the mirlitons. Later, in a month or two when I publish my cookbook, you can sell them in your booth. What do you think?" Leslie said.

"Great idea. I'll be happy to promote and sell your books," Ben told her.

Just then a woman about Ben's age or a little older walked behind the counter of the booth. She appeared to have had a hard life with a frown covering her wrinkled sun-damaged face and her gray hair tied back in a bun. Never smiling or saying hello she sat down in a lawn chair behind where Ben was standing helping customers. Ben turned around and motioned for her to come to the counter.

"Leslie, this is my sister. Mary, this is the lady I told you about. She is an author and she is putting together a cookbook," he said making sure Mary understood who she was talking to.

"Hello Mary, this is my husband Sidney," Lesley said, extending her hand.

Mary shook her hand and nodded toward Sidney in acknowledgment. Never smiling, she returned to her chair and began to fan herself with a paper fan on a stick advertising The French Market.

"It's nice to have help in your space, especially on a busy day like this," Sidney told Ben.

"She's pretty tired right now. She just came from a birthing," he said.

Sidney looked at Leslie with a questioning look.

The Cookbook

"You must be a midwife," Leslie said to Mary. "Was it a boy or a girl?"

"Neither, it was stillborn," Mary said quietly.

"Oh, how sad. Is the mother alright?"

"Yeah, physically, emotionally she's a wreck," Mary said

"I can only imagine and it must take a toll on you too," Leslie told her with empathy. "I would like to pray for her. What is her name?"

"Thank you, her name is Olivia," Mary said smiling for the first time at Leslie's kindness.

"And I will pray for you too, Mary," she said smiling at her.

Sidney paid for the vegetables they bought from Ben. It was mostly types of potatoes they didn't grow in their garden. As they walked away Sidney took Leslie's hand and squeezed it. He loved her so much and her acts of kindness made his heart swell. Sometimes they didn't have to say a word to each other. They had been together long enough to understand what each other felt. Leslie looked up at her handsome husband and smiled.

Later that evening they relaxed after a busy day that started with working in their garden and ended with preparing fresh veggies for their dinner.

"Sid that was undoubtedly the best steak we've had in a while. You did a great job on the grill. I've missed your grilling skills lately. I'm glad you're into it again," Lesley said, giving him a hug.

"Yeah, me too. There's nothing quite like a good grilled steak unless it is some of your excellent creations from your kitchen," he said hugging her back. "So this midwife thing. What exactly does a midwife do?"

"Pearl's mother is pregnant and she gives birth at home with a midwife instead of having a doctor present at the hospital. Her mother has had five babies with a midwife at home," Leslie said shaking her head. "I could never do that and she isn't young. Pearl was born at home when her mother was only fifteen. So she must be in her late thirties because Pearl has to be at least twenty-four, either way, it is scary."

"It sure sounds risky. I'm so glad you had Ryan at the hospital. That was stressful enough, but to have a baby at home? Wow, I don't think I would be in favor of that."

"It was nice having Ryan pop in unexpectedly the other evening on a school night," Leslie commented.

"Yes, it was," Sidney replied hoping it wouldn't go any further.

"He seemed to be anxious to talk to you about something. Is everything okay?"

"Yeah, I think so. You know how young people are they blow everything out of proportion. I think he just needed to talk to his old man. But he's okay, nothing to worry about. Didn't you say you had made a dessert?" he said changing the subject.

"I did. It's a twist on strawberry shortcake. I think you'll like it and it is heart-healthy," she said getting up and going to the kitchen. She felt good about Ryan being able to come to his dad with concerns however she sensed there was more to the story. But, since Sidney chose not to elaborate on his meeting with Ryan she would let it pass for now.

Chapter 15

About a week later Leslie waited for Annabelle upstairs where brunch was served at Brennan's on Royal Street. The two decided to change it up a little and meet for brunch instead of their usual lunch date. The enticing aroma filled the air around her increasing her appetite as she scanned the menu. Sipping on a cup of pressed coffee she ordered earlier, she saw Annabelle coming up the stairs in her usual attire — wide-brimmed hat, white gloves, and a strikingly attractive black and white dress, cinched in at the waist, showing off her hourglass figure.

"Well, hello gorgeous," Leslie said in her brightly printed waist dress and canvas shoes, feeling under dressed, as usual, when she was around Annabelle.

"And you look gorgeous too as always," Annabelle said quite sincerely.

Molly Owen

She ordered a cup of pressed coffee when the waiter, that followed her to the table stood in anticipation of their order.

"This was a great idea. Jeffrey and I used to come here all the time. Now that life is so hectic with the twins we are lucky to be able to go across the street to the bakery," she said putting her hat and gloves on the chair beside her.

"Oh, Annabelle, I love that short hairdo on you, " Leslie remarked.

"Thank you. It's different alright, I haven't quite gotten used to it," she said.

"Well, with your thick black hair, you can pull it off. I wouldn't be able to keep it like that for five minutes. My hair is just not thick enough," Leslie said, then realized the hair conversation had ended. "What's on your mind?"

"Oh, a lot of things. What are you getting?"

"I thought the Pain Perdu sounded good. I'm in the mood for a big thick slice of fried French bread soaked in yummy batter with lots of butter," Leslie said salivating. "I know this sounds terrible but once in a while, I have to indulge. I'm so good at sticking to Sidney's heart diet most of the time."

"How is he doing in his new office?"

"Really well and I like having him close by. I think Charles is more comfortable with it as well."

"I'm glad it's working out. I'm not at home as much as you are but I like thinking of Jeffrey being close, especially when the girls are home."

"Not to change the subject, however, I've been thinking about something lately and I want to see what you think?" Leslie said.

The Cookbook

Distracted by the waiter as she asked some questions about items on the menu, Annabelle stopped listening. After she and Leslie ordered, Annabelle asked her to repeat what she had been saying.

"I just want your opinion on something," Leslie said, again noticing Annabelle's mood.

"Okay."

"I have an idea, now that the garden is mature, we can share the bounty with others. Those who want to help plant and weed are welcome, but the harvest is there to share. Perhaps we can set aside a time, when each crop comes in, for picking. Each family could bring a basket and go through the garden picking vegetables," Leslie said.

"I think that's a great idea. So just anybody or would you limit it to people you know?"

"I thought to start it with the Sunday prayer group, then others as we saw the need. What do you think?" Leslie said taking a bite of the pain perdu. "This is so good Annabelle, here take a bite," she said passing her plate over to her.

"That is good, thanks," she said taking a bite.

"Are you okay? You seem far away. Is it a case you're working on? You just don't seem yourself," Leslie said continuing to devour her food. "I'm going to have to come up with my version of Pain Perdu but I don't think I can beat this." Then she looked at Annabelle and realized she was close to tears.

"What's wrong?" Leslie asked wiping her mouth with a napkin.

With a big sigh, Annabelle put her fork down and looked Leslie straight in the eye and asked. "How's Ryan these days?"

"He's okay. Why do you ask?" Leslie said giving Annabelle her full attention.

"And Karlah?"

"What's this about? You're scaring me." Leslie said.

"What do you know about the situation with Sarah's father?" she quizzed waiting for Leslie to respond.

"Sarah? Sarah who?" Leslie said beginning to get a little angry.

"Sarah, in the gymnastics class with Jamie and Amy,"

"Annabelle, I don't have a clue as to what you are talking about. I don't even know a Sarah in the girl's gymnastics class, should I?" Leslie adjusted herself in her chair.

"Her father's name is Harry, Harry Burke," Annabelle said.

Leslie could feel her face go hot as she tried to put something together to make sense out of the questions Annabelle was throwing at her.

"What about him?" she said with the same tone that her friend was using.

"Then you do know everything. How could you keep this from me? You are as bad as Jeffrey. Do you think after all these years and everything we have been through together that I wouldn't be capable of handling this kind of situation?"

Swallowing hard, Leslie took a deep cleansing breath. Softy, she said, "Annabelle, I don't know what you are accusing me of, can we start at the beginning?"

"Didn't Ryan come to your house a few days ago and talk to Sidney?"

"Yes. But, what does this have to do with Karlah?"

"Right after he talked to Sidney he came straight to our house and he and Jeffrey went to Jeffrey's office and had quite a discussion."

"About what?" Leslie said more frustrated than before.

"Are you telling me you don't know that Sarah's father, Harry Burke, has been stocking Karlah, following her, staring at her and scaring her to the point that she told Ryan about it. That Harry was waiting for Karlah outside her dorm in the rain."

"No. No, I didn't know any of that. Sidney and Charles asked me to help run a background check on Harry. That's all. They didn't tell me why or even who the background check was for. All I found was the name of his first wife and baby girl. They both died in childbirth. I didn't know and still don't know why Sidney was investigating Harry. But now that you've told me this, it makes sense. But why is Ryan involved?"

Annabelle began to tell Leslie what Jeffrey had told her. She automatically assumed that Leslie knew all about it and hadn't shared it with her. As the two of them began to put it together tears were running down both of their faces.

"It's not enough that this is messing with my marriage, but now it is messing with my relationship with my best friend. I'm so sorry Leslie, please forgive me," Annabelle asked her friend.

"There is nothing to forgive. We are both in the dark evidently about the real reason for this investigation. When I told Sidney that Harry's first wife died in childbirth and that the baby didn't live either he asked me if I find out anything about the travel agency she, by the way, her name was Patricia, owned. Then he told me he had found out that Harry's second wife was the listing agent for Patricia's travel agency when Harry decided to sell it after he lost her and their baby."

"How sad is that? I met Jennifer, his second wife, and Sarah's mother. Remember I told you about her. She is a piece of work. She made me very uncomfortable when she recognized me as Jonathon's attorney and she talked about the trial like it was yesterday, down to the very detail, some of which I didn't remember."

"Well, I don't know about you, but there is more to this story than we are privy to, don't you agree?"

"Oh, I'm sure of it. Jeffrey knows something that he told me he couldn't share because of confidentiality." Annabelle confided in Leslie.

"So that's the key. Whatever Jeffrey knows could break this wide open, don't you think? I mean all the rest of it seems pretty simple,"

"Harry did tell Jeffrey, when we were in Houston, about his first wife and baby. Jeffrey said he almost cried talking about them. So I asked him how does a man like that, loving husband and father, goes after a young thing like Karlah. That's when he told me there was more to it that he could not share with me. I was so angry with him. This involves our girls. What if something awful were too happened to Karlah? It would devastate the twins."

"Well at least Sidney and Charles are on top of it now and I'm going to talk to Sidney about not telling me the whole story but he may not know the whole story either, Annabelle. I'll find out how much he knows. I'm so sorry about all of this. Please know,

Annabelle, if I knew anything that would affect your family, I would tell you," Leslie told her getting up and hugging her.

"I'm sorry, Leslie, I should have known you wouldn't keep something like this from me. You were just as much in the dark as I was. I think it is time we let our men know that we won't be kept in the dark again about things that affect our two families and they might as well get used to it."

"Pray with me," Leslie said, *"Father, you are the king of kings and you see all and know all. We ask that the situation with Karlah be resolved and she is safe. Bless this friendship and help our husbands understand our needs in situations like this. I pray for Ryan in this too, God, that he is able to help Karlah and support her through this. In Jesus' Name. Amen."*

Chapter 16

Jeffrey asked Harry to meet him at the same place as before and told him they needed to talk. As he waited in a dark corner of the café, he became concerned that Harry wasn't going to show up. Thirty minutes had passed when Harry finally walked through the door of the café. Jeffrey rose to let him know where he was sitting.

"I had almost given up on you," Jeffrey said.

"Sorry, I was having a hard time getting away. Jennifer is wanting to do some remodeling and she had the contractor there. Anyway, I'm here now. What is so urgent?"

"Harry, I'm afraid I can't respect the confidentiality I promised you any longer," Jeffrey said quite frankly.

"What do you mean? Has something happened?"

"Yes, you showed up at Karlah's dorm, in the rain the other night. What were you thinking? If your suspensions are correct then we need to pursue it. But, this behavior can't go on, Harry. You scared her to the point that she told her friend, Ryan, what you've been up to. Ryan talked to his father and then came to me."

"Why did he come to you?"

"Because Karlah asked me to check you out and I promised her I would. I asked Ryan's father to do a background check on you," Jeffrey confessed.

Harry sat stunned. He had no idea that he had caused Karlah so much pain. He wasn't sure what he was doing that night in the rain but he wanted to ask her something anything that would ease his pain. Perhaps it was time to find some answers but he didn't know where to begin.

"Ryan's father? Is he some kind of a detective?" Harry asked.

"Yes, he owns Rye Detective Service. He is a private investigator and used to be with the FBI."

"So, do you think he could investigate the situation? Maybe he would prove me wrong. But, Jeffrey, I have to know. It's driving me crazy," Harry confided in him.

"Why don't you talk to Sidney, the detective? I can introduce you to him. Because I asked him to do a background check on you, he already has information about your first wife and the baby you lost. So, he could start from there," Jeffrey said.

"Okay, do you think he would see me now before I lose my nerve?"

"Let me check," he said listening for Sidney to answer on his cell phone. "Hey, Sidney, I'm here with Harry and he wants to talk to you about something you may be able to help him with. Are you free now to see him? Great, we'll be there soon. Thanks," Jeffrey told Sidney.

*****

"Well, now, maybe we will get to the bottom of this mystery," Sidney said to Charles. "That was Jeffrey and he is bringing Harry here to talk to us about something he needs help with."

"I don't know Sidney, I don't see how we can help him with his problem. He needs a counselor of some sort," Charles said.

"Well, let's see what he has to say," Sidney said. "At least Leslie won't be popping in. She and Annabelle are meeting for Brunch."

Jeffrey opened the door and invited Harry inside to meet Charles and Sidney. The men shook hands and Sidney asked Harry to sit across from him at his desk. Jeffrey sat at Charles's desk and waited for Harry to share his situation.

"I don't know where to begin. Jeffrey said you know about my wife and my baby girl," Harry said.

"Yes. They died in childbirth," Sidney said confirming his knowledge of the reason for their death.

"Well, and please understand this is not my usual behavior, the first time I took my daughter Sarah to Gymnastic class and met her instructor, Karlah, well it nearly took my breath away," he said, trying to keep his composure. "If I didn't know better I would have thought…my deceased wife was standing in front of me."

"So, you're saying that Karlah looks like Patricia?" Sidney asked.

"How did you know her name was Patricia?" Then he remembered, "Oh. Jeffrey told me you were doing a background check on me," Harry said.

"So go on. Karlah looks like your first wife," Sidney encouraged him to continue.

"Not only looks but down to her mannerisms, her smile, everything about her is a carbon copy of my wife. You see, Patricia and I were high school sweethearts, and we got married right out of high school," Harry said hoping Sidney believed him.

"Okay, so what are you saying?" Sidney asked.

"I'm hoping that this is where you come in. I never saw my baby girl. I was told that she was stillborn and I never questioned it. At the time, I was devastated over the loss of my wife and I guess I wasn't thinking straight. Anyway, I just accepted what I was told."

"So the hospital made the arrangements," Sidney said puzzled.

"Oh, she didn't give birth at the hospital. She gave birth with a midwife. When we found out she was pregnant, she insisted on giving birth at home with a midwife. I begged her to reconsider and go to the hospital. However, it became such an issue with us that I stopped bringing it up. I was at a client's in Lafayette when she went into labor, early, two weeks before the baby was due. She called me crying and said she had already called the midwife. I begged her to call an ambulance and go to the hospital but she wouldn't listen. I tried but I didn't get there in time." Harry said showing emotion.

"What happened when you did get there?" Sidney asked gently knowing how the memories of that day must hurt.

The Cookbook

"No one was there. I didn't know where they were. I couldn't believe it. I was in shock. I didn't know what to do," Harry said almost in tears.

Sidney got up and walked to the coffee pot. He offered a cup to Harry.

"Thank You, I take it black," he said. Then taking the cup he took a sip as he waited for Sidney to react to this new information.

Sidney stood next to him as he mulled the information over in his mind. *Could Harry be trying to replace his dead wife or daughter? Or was this something that needed investigating. It happened over twenty years ago. Could what Harry believes to have really happened to be in fact what really happened? Somehow, did his daughter live.... But, how could that be? One of the first things to do would be to get a DNA sample from Karlah. She would have to consent, and that would put her in a tailspin. She believes she was raised by her own mother,* Sidney surmised as he walked back around his desk and took a seat.

"Well, Harry, this is quite the dilemma. Karlah believes she was raised by her birth mother who by the way is deceased, so she can't shed any light on the subject. Her father died while her mother was pregnant with her. Why don't you let Charles and I sort this out and figure out where to begin."

"So, you're going to help me? You believe me?" Harry said standing up and putting the cup of coffee back by the coffee pot.

"Yes, I'm not sure why, but I believe you," Sidney said standing up and shaking his hand.

Jeffrey got up and thanked Sidney and he and Harry made their way to the door. Sidney stopped them.

Molly Owen

"Harry, I would like to say a prayer with you." And putting his hand on Harry's Shoulder he began to pray *"Almighty God our heavenly Father we come to ask that you ease Harry's pain. Help us, Father, to help him in his grief which is still a major part of his daily living. We ask for peace, give him strength, Jesus, and guide his actions. We also pray for Karlah as we go forward with this investigation that you will be with her and give her strength and courage. All these things we pray in Jesus' Name. Amen."*

Then patting Harry's shoulder, he told him he would stay in touch and said goodbye. Jeffrey put his hand out and shook Sidney's hand again thanking him.

After they were out of earshot, Sidney turned to Charles and shook his head. "Boy, that really got to me. Can you imagine the pain that man is in?" he said sitting back down at his desk and clasping his hands behind his head he leaned back in his chair.

"You can say that again. At least we now know why he can't stay away from her. Do you really believe that Karlah may be his daughter?" Charles said quite truthfully.

"What I'm having trouble understanding is how this could happen in reality. If she was at a hospital it could be a matter of switched babies but in a home birth situation? How could that happen? The baby was stillborn according to everything Harry was told. Of course, he wasn't present at the birth and that very fact gives me hope and is the only thing that has me wanting to seek the truth," Sidney told Charles sitting back up and making some notes on a scratchpad.

"That's all well and good, but where do we start?" Charles asked.

"With the birth certificates. Every birth has to be recorded. I'm going to have to clue Leslie in on this because she can be a big help," he said.

Just then his cell rang. Looking at the caller ID, he saw it was Jeffrey. He answered thinking maybe he would tell him something Harry had left out. But Jeffrey had decided Annabelle and Leslie needed to be told of the latest development because of Ryan's involvement at this point.

"I don't know what to tell you about that. But, if Ryan knows what's going on before we tell Karlah, he could have a slip of the tongue," Jeffrey told Sidney.

"I thought about that, too. I planned to tell Leslie because, like I told Charles, she can be a big help with this and you know if Leslie knows then we better tell Annabelle," Sidney said.

"My thought exactly, I did bring Annabelle up to speed about the reason Ryan came over the other night. She was very upset with me for not telling her sooner. At that time, I was the only one that knew what Harry was thinking. But now that you know, I think it's safe to tell them," he said.

"I agree. I'll tell Leslie tonight," Sidney said.

"Sidney, I don't think Harry is a believer, but he was moved that you said a prayer for him. He told me he wasn't used to anyone praying for him. So thank you, I appreciate what you did and the fact you are willing to see if you can help him. I know it is a tall order, but with God's help I pray you can get to the bottom of this for Harry's peace of mind, for that matter, Karlah's peace of mind," Jeffrey told him.

*****

That evening, after the dishes were cleaned and put away, Sidney poured two cups of coffee and asked Leslie to join him in their living room. She sat down next to him and, leaning over, gave him a kiss.

"This is nice, just the two of us relaxing after a long day. Sid, I have something I want to talk to you about, it's concerning Harry Burke," she said.

"Well, that's interesting, because I want to talk to you on the same subject," Sidney told her.

"You go first," Leslie said getting comfortable and looking at her husband in anticipation of what he was about to say.

Sidney told her about Harry's visit that morning and how he needed her to help to investigate the possibility that Karlah was his daughter. He explained the fact that there was not much to go on, but Harry needed to know one way or the other.

Leslie sat stunned by what Sidney told her. "It changes my whole concept of the situation," she told Sidney. "Why do we do that? We are so willing to judge someone, without giving them the benefit of the doubt. We are so willing to just accept surface things and don't think beyond. Oh, Sid, what about Karlah?"

"Jeffrey has assured me that Harry will be careful around Karlah, especially now that he knows the harm he has caused her," Sidney said.

"And Ryan. What are we going to tell Ryan?" she said concerned.

"Ryan can't know at this point. Jeffrey and I are going to impress on Ryan that Harry will leave her alone," he assured her.

"Speaking of Jeffrey, I sure hope he shares this new information with Annabelle. At our brunch today, she told me she was very upset that Jeffrey had not shared Karlah's concern about Harry. And she accused me of knowing more than I knew. It was sad, Sid. It could have broken any trust that she and I have with each other," Leslie said almost in tears.

Sidney put his arms around her and told her how sorry he was that this had come between their friendships. "Jeffrey was the only one who knew the truth behind Harry's actions. I was unaware of this until today. And yes, he is probably telling Annabelle as we speak," Sidney told her putting her at ease.

Chapter **17**

The mirlitons were weighing the trellis down, nearly to the ground, causing Ryan and Sidney to have to stabilize it with rebar and 2x4 boards. Today was Saturday, and the three of them were working hard in the garden where a plethora of vegetables covered every plant.

Tomorrow, at our prayer meeting, I'm going to give everyone a sack and invite them to help themselves to any of the vegetables in the garden. We will never be able to use all of this. I can just freeze and can so much," Leslie said.

"I never thought it would produce this much. Did you, mom?" Ryan said walking between rows of peppers.

"To be honest, I didn't. I think we may have over planted. But it's okay, now others can share. And who knows? That may have been God's plan all along," she said with a smile.

Ryan loved his mom's positive attitude. Her relationship with God was part of who she was and it gave him peace knowing that. He felt fortunate to have parents who kept God at the center of their lives. This is the way he was raised and it guided him in his life. He knew he was a sinner and he constantly thanked his heavenly Father for His grace through His Son Jesus Christ. When events happened, good and bad, he was assured that with God by his side he would be able to handle it. This was becoming very clear when talking to his dad about Karlah's situation.

"I promise, dad," he told Sidney after their talk about reassuring Karlah and making sure she could trust Jeffrey and Sidney when told they had talked to Harry and he would leave her alone.

At the Sunday meeting, Leslie announced her plan to have everyone share in the bounty from her garden. She laid a stack of paper bags on the table and told everyone to help themselves. After the prayer time, many of the people thanked Leslie for her generous offer as they took a sack and went out the back door to the garden.

"What a wonderful idea, Leslie, and now I see why," Annabelle said starting to fill her sack.

"Did Jeffrey give you a heads up on the confusion we talked about at brunch?" Leslie asked when they were away from the rest of the pickers.

"He did, can you believe it. It is just so sad for everyone involved," she said.

"I know, I feel that way too. I'm going to help Sid and Charles with some research. I don't really hope to find out much considering the circumstances," Leslie said handing her a couple of mirlitons.

"You mean because of the midwife thing?" she asked.

The Cookbook

"Yes, but I may have a place to start with someone who is a midwife."

"Leslie, what on earth are these?" she said holding the green ugly twisted vegetables in her hands.

"Those are the mirlitons I told you about. They are like squash. I'll give you some recipes," she said laughing at the expression on Annabelle's face as she held them at arm's length in front of her.

"They are really ugly, aren't they?"

"Yes, but they are really good when prepared right," Leslie assured her.

"Well, I'm not as good of a cook as you are so we'll see," she confessed. "I wonder why Karlah didn't come today."

"Ryan said she had a cold and was going to stay in the dorm and see if she could shake it off before class on Monday."

*****

After breakfast, Sidney took his cup of coffee out to his office. It was a warm, humid day with a storm brewing in the gulf. The air hung heavy and Sidney noticed he was having a hard time breathing. Once inside with the air conditioning, he put his cup down and went to his desk. Sitting down in his chair he took some deep cleansing breaths and began to feel better. He convinced himself that it was because of the high humidity and began to write down some ideas he had about the Harry Burke case.

He had Leslie searching for midwives at the time Patricia gave birth, and Charles was headed for the Barataria Basin, to the place where Harry and Patricia lived. Sidney wanted him to check out the public records of marriage licenses, birth certificates, and any information he could find on the travel agency Patricia owned.

"Maybe find out if anyone still lives in the neighborhood where they lived and see if they remember anything," he had told Charles.

"I better plan to stay overnight," Charles confirmed with Sidney.

*****

Sidney was surprised when Leslie came through the door with their lunch. He looked up and cleared a place on his desk.

"Have you heard from Charles?" Leslie asked

"Not a word. He will probably call later this afternoon," Sidney said taking a bite of the sandwich. "How are you coming with your research? Did you look up Ben's sister Mary?"

"Yes, I was surprised to learn that she isn't even a nurse as far as I can find out. I was always under the impression that midwives had to have some nurse training. I want to get more information about the legal ramifications that may help me in my search. I must admit there aren't too many midwives registered in or around Barataria now, or back then. One thing's for sure, Mary isn't registered at all. Everything I found out about her puts her under the radar. I wonder how many other unregistered midwives there are in Barataria Basin?" she told Sidney gathering up their lunch dishes.

"It seems as if a pregnant mother can hire a certified nurse-midwife to attend a birth in a hospital setting but in several states, they have no licensing laws so practicing midwives are breaking the law because they are practicing medicine without a license. Even though in some states it is illegal to have a

The Cookbook

midwife for a home birth, but, it's not illegal to give birth at home unassisted. But at that point it is up to the mother in order to get a birth certificate to have the baby examined by a doctor or midwife soon after the birth," she told him.

"Could it be that the midwife wasn't present for the delivery. That could be why Patricia died. But if she had a live birth... where did the stillbirth baby come from? I don't know, Les, it is all very confusing. I have tried to figure that out from the beginning. However, your information puts a different light on things," Sidney told her. "Harry said when his wife told him she was in labor she had called the midwife."

"If the baby was early, it could have been very small or there was a miscalculation as to the due date. I've heard that happening," Leslie said trying to come up with a believable scenario.

"Keep digging, you're bound to find something," he said.

Sidney told her he needed her to stay on top of it because something wasn't right, if what Harry had told them was true, and Sidney had no reason to believe it wasn't. Then they were missing something. Something very important.

Later that afternoon, when Charles called, he told Sidney he was staying in Harvey about ten miles from Barataria.

"There are no hospitals in Barataria," he said. "So, she would have had to travel to Harvey to deliver at a hospital, but there is no record of a baby being born or brought to the hospital here on that date."

"How about hospital certificates?"

"So far I've had no luck there either," Charles told him. "This is a very small community of people, so someone has to know something. Tomorrow I'm going to talk to neighbors and maybe check with clergy and the priest."

"Good idea, keep in touch," Sidney told him.

The Cookbook

Chapter **18**

The room filled with chattering students warming up for their lesson. The twins were talking to Sarah while their mothers stood off to the side watching.

"Where is their teacher?" Jennifer stated for everyone to hear.

"I heard she wasn't feeling well. She may not be here today," Annabelle said hoping to give Karlah the benefit of the doubt.

"Well finally, there she is. I can't stay and this has been very inconvenient," Jennifer said getting her things from the chair behind her in preparation to leave.

"Is Harry alright?" Annabelle asked concerned.

"He is fine just impossible," she said. "Why do you ask?"

"Well, it's just that he usually brings Sarah," Annabelle tells her.

Molly Owen

"Not today. He insisted I bring her, something about a client. He seems to forget that I have clients, and I can't be running Sarah everywhere. This is his job, we agreed," she said turning and walking toward the exit.

"Oh, hello Mrs. Burke. Nice to see you again," Karlah said as Jennifer acknowledges her with a wave of the hand not saying a word as she hurried out the door.

Maybe Ryan was right. Karlah thought to herself as she rounded up the students. She was aware that Sarah's mother had never brought Sarah to class. So, maybe this was a step in the right direction, and she wouldn't have to deal with Mr. Burke any more.

After class, Annabelle noticed that Sarah was waiting for a ride. Everyone else was gone except Sarah and the twins. Jamie and Amy were helping Karlah put supplies away.

"Do you need a ride?" Annabelle asked Sarah.

"I hope my mom didn't forget she was supposed to pick me up after class," Sarah said embarrassed.

"Don't worry I can take you home if you need a ride," Annabelle assured her, wondering why Jennifer wasn't there.

*****

"It was so uncomfortable for Sarah, I felt sorry for her. Jennifer never showed up, so the girls and I waited outside until Harry came for her. Karlah had to lock up the gym so she could get to her class," Annabelle told Leslie.

"What you said earlier about her not being the motherly type is very apparent," Leslie commented.

The Cookbook

"So are you having any luck on finding a trail that leads to solving this mystery?"

"No. I've hit a dead-end and so I'm back working on my cookbook. I want to get it published and on the shelves in a couple of months. By the way, did you try the recipe with the mirlitons?" Leslie asked.

"Actually, I did and I was pleasantly surprised at how good it was. Even the girls liked it and believe me that is saying something. Of course, they didn't know what was in it or it could have been a different story," she said laughing. "I guess it is no different than using other squash, like zucchini, or even yellow squash."

"Yes, I'm always tricking my men. But they have gotten to the point where they ask what's in it before taking a bite. The other night I served them, Cajun boudin. You know like you order in restaurants. It's usually a sausage put into casings. But, I made meatballs out of the pre-casing mixture. It was really good and Sidney couldn't believe it was the same thing," Leslie told her.

After their conversation, Leslie couldn't get Jennifer off her mind. Somehow Jennifer was a part of this mystery. However, she had found nothing to indicate her involvement except that she was the listing agent when Harry decided to sell the travel agency. Staring out the window her thoughts went back to what Annabelle had told her about Jennifer not being the motherly type. *Then why did they have a child?* Then she wondered *how long they had been married.* She decided to see if she could get some answers to those questions. Opening her laptop, she searched for records starting with Harry's second marriage.

Then something stood out as she again ran across information on the travel agency. Even though Jennifer was a Realtor in New Orleans, she sold commercial as well as residential real estate and she was the listing agent for the travel agency in Barataria that sold to Patricia and Harry. Leslie found the listing for the agency in the New Orleans newspaper archives. *Were the Burkes married in New Orleans or Barataria?* She asked herself. "Looks like they were married in New Orleans," she said out loud, bringing up the Marriage Certificate. *So, did they know Jennifer before?* These were all questions Lesley planned to share with Sidney.

*****

"So don't you think it strange that she was the one who sold them the travel agency? She must have been very new as a Realtor. She was probably still in her early twenties. Not much older than Patricia and Harry were at the time. Did one or the other of them come from money?" Leslie kept asking Sidney.

"Well, to your first question, this whole thing is strange. As for one, or both of them coming from money, I think it is a strong possibility. They went to a private Catholic school together. I think Harry made reference to growing up in the French Quarter. So, I don't know, they would have had to either have money or very good credit to buy the travel agency at such a young age."

"They were only married a year or so before Patricia died. No wonder Harry is so sure that Karlah is his daughter. Didn't you say she looks like Patricia? That would be hard," Leslie said.

"Why don't you follow the money angle? It just might lead us somewhere, and while we're at it, let's do more checking on Jennifer and her finances at the time," Sidney said, still trying to put things together.

Chapter 19

"I thought we had an agreement, Harry, if Sarah got involved in any extracurricular activity you would be in charge of getting her to and from," Jennifer scolded him.

"Yes, but there are times when that is not possible, and now is that time. Surely you can rearrange your schedule to help out with this. I have managed to rearrange mine."

"Did you know the teacher, that Karlah person, was late and that made me late? By the way, there is something about that girl, I can't put my finger on it, it gives me the creeps," Jennifer said shaking her whole body in disgust.

"What do you mean?" Harry asked surprised at her reaction. It had occurred to him that she may see the resemblance as he did.

"I don't know," she answered.

"Well, perhaps I can ask Annabelle Bordeaux if Sarah can get a ride with them?" he said thinking it would be better than Jennifer putting two and two together. As far as Harry knew she had only seen Karlah a couple of times.

"There, you see, you can find another answer if you try," she told him getting her purse and leaving.

Harry wished she spent more time with Sarah. His daughter was at the age where she needed to be able to talk to her mother. Jennifer had never been the nurturing type. Sometimes he wondered if it had been wise on his part to talk her into having a child. He so desperately wanted to be a father that he didn't think about what it would be like for the child. He did his best to give Sarah enough love and support for two parents but she was acutely aware of her mother's absence. Jennifer wasn't around much for him, let alone Sarah.

When Sarah came into the world, he was elated. However, Jennifer couldn't wait to get back to work, and immediately turned all responsibility of the baby over to him. "After all," she had told him. "This is what you wanted and at least it didn't kill me as it did your first wife."

Sitting at his desk, he stared out the window at the sunset and remembered how excited he and Patricia were at the prospect of having many children. They had been so pleased to find out she was pregnant, unlike Jennifer who found the whole thing disgusting.

Children had never been part of Jennifer's plans. Money was her motivation, and no one would get in the way of that, not even her own child. The marriage had been rough from the beginning. As the years went by, they drew further apart. She wanted wealth, and all it brought with it. At the time they bought their home in the Garden District, it was a real struggle, financially. Harry remembered how Jennifer had been very disappointed when they couldn't afford the Bordeaux estate. She had accused Katrina Louise Bordeaux of making it impossible for them to get the place she so desperately wanted.

Jeffrey's sister Katrina Louise, a well-known Realtor in New Orleans, had been Jennifer's rival from the beginning of her career. That is why she had been so interested in Jonathon Bordeaux's trial. Her hope had been that the Bordeaux reputation would have been so tainted by the results of the trial that Katrina Louise would not be able to keep her clientele and she could swoop right in and take over.

That night in Houston when Jennifer went on and on about the trial, and the fact that she knew so much about Annabelle, was all a show. She desperately wanted in the same crowd that the Robicheaux and Bordeaux families enjoyed. That would be a dream come true for Jennifer. The youngest of eight children, she struggled to get ahead. Growing up in a very poor family, she was the only one that managed to make anything of herself. She took the brokers test twice and barely passed. Then managed to get a job with a real estate company selling commercial property. One of the other Realtors in her office gave her the listing for the travel agency in Barataria to help her get started. That was how she met Harry and Patricia.

There were times when Harry questioned why he was married to Jennifer. After Patricia died Jennifer moved right into his life and before he realized what was happening she was planning their wedding. He had moved back to the French Quarter which made it more convenient for Jennifer to pursue him.

The one good thing that came out of his marriage to Jennifer was his daughter Sarah, the love of his life. If he found out that Karlah was also his daughter he would feel blessed two-fold.

"Harry?"

"What," he answered.

"Harry, I have been calling you from the kitchen. What are you doing just sitting here in the dark?" Jennifer asked.

"Just thinking, I didn't know you were home," he answered.

"About what? What are you thinking about Harry?"

"Nothing, you wouldn't understand if I told you," Harry said

"Then don't tell me. It's probably not important anyway,"

"Have you ever gone to church?" he asked

"No. And I don't intend to go now if that's what you were thinking. What's gotten into you anyway?"

"Something's missing in our lives, Jennifer," he said softly.

"And you think it's church? I thought we gave up all of that nonsense a long time ago," she said

"As I recall I was the one giving it up. I was raised in the church but since you weren't I gave it up because you didn't like me going. I think it would be good for Sarah," Harry told her.

"Then by all means go, take her, just leave me out of it," she said turning and leaving the room.

Yes, he would talk to her about it in the morning, he promised himself.

*****

"Why don't we go to the Rye's where the twins go? They have invited me to go with them several times," Sarah told her father at the breakfast table the next morning.

The Cookbook

Jennifer overheard their conversation and said, "That's a great idea, Harry we could all go to the Rye's little bible study."

"I thought you weren't interested," Harry said surprised.

"Well, I've changed my mind," she said pouring herself another cup of coffee.

Jennifer was willing to do anything to get into the upper-class circle, even if she had to go to church. Always, her main goal in life was to be accepted in groups above the life she came from. She would do what it took to better her position in society.

Chapter **20**

For some reason, Ryan had been thinking about Karlah all day. He had a break between classes this afternoon, and decided to call Karlah to see if she wanted to meet him later in the Student Lounge... just to talk.

"That would be really nice, Ryan, but I have to teach at the gym later," she told him.

"So when are you through with that?"

"Around six, but don't you need to study?" she said.

"Yes, and I guess you do too. So let's meet for a bite to eat and study later. What do you say?"

"Well, okay," she said looking at the clock.

"We can still meet at the Student Lounge, I'll pick up something for our dinner. What are you in the mood for?"

"I'll let you surprise me."

"Now you're talking dangerous, I go for spicy. The hotter the better," he said laughing.

"So do I. That will be just fine. Whatever you get. I'll see you a little after six in the Student Lounge," she said hanging up the phone and hurrying out the door to class.

Balancing his books and carrying their dinner, he managed to get through the door. He scanned the room and found Karlah sitting back in a corner under an overhead light. She turned and smiled as she stood up and helped him with his load. Setting their dinner down she opened the bag and peered inside.

"Yummy. Smells good. Let me guess. Shrimp Creole?"

"Yep. Is that okay? It's pretty spicy."

As they prepared to eat, Ryan reached over and took her hand. "Let's pray. *Father, we are so blessed by your grace that surrounds us daily. Thank you for this beautiful day and for our friends. Bless this food for the nourishment of our bodies. In Jesus' Name. Amen.*" Then giving her hand a squeeze, he let go.

Their conversation flowed like they had been friends forever. They joked about familiar things and he teased her when her eyes were watering after a few bites of the spiciest Shrimp Creole either one had ever experienced. He confessed to ordering it extra spicy and she laughed at him as his face turned red after he tried a few bites. He got up and went to the drink machine and came back to the table with drinks to put out the fire. They gulped the drinks down until the cans were empty then turning to face each other they began to laugh again.

The Cookbook

"I like your hair like that," he said gathering the bowls, spoons, napkins, putting them in the sack and carrying it to the trash can.

"Thank you, this is my gym hairdo,"

"Well, I like it," he said, not sure why it needed to be said again.

Getting their books out they prepared to study. They were silent as each was deep in thought, taking notes and reading page after page. An hour had gone by, and Ryan sat up and stretched. Looking over at Karlah he thought, *she sure is cute. Why had he not noticed that before?* He asked himself. About that time Karlah caught him staring at her and smiled.

"Are you finished studying? Or just taking a break," she asked.

"Just taking a break. How about you?"

"Yeah, I'm at a stopping point. It is hard to believe this semester will soon be over. What are your plans for the summer?" she asked.

"I hadn't thought much about it. How about you?"

"I need to find a job for the summer just to make ends meet," she confessed.

"You're not going to teach Gymnastics?"

"Maybe, if I get enough students. By the way, Mrs. Burke brought Sarah to class last week. And this week, Sarah came with the twins. So, I guess you were right about Mr. Bordeaux talking to Mr. Burke. Thank you for helping me with that situation, Ryan," she said. "I really appreciate it."

"No problem, I'm glad to help. I want you to feel free to call me any time you have a problem," Ryan said raising an eyebrow. "Are you coming to prayer meeting Sunday?"

"I plan on it," she said.

"How about I give you a ride?"

"Okay," she said.

And with that, they went back to studying.

Chapter 21

Sidney was preparing his lesson for Sunday morning while Ryan and Leslie worked in the garden. For some reason, he had chosen forgiveness as his subject. Many verses in scripture address forgiveness, and he was aware it was a hard subject to deal with sometimes.

He remembered Leslie's battle with it when she found out about Nick, her father, Ryan's grandfather. Even though she forgave her father, the pain lingered, coming back to haunt her as she would remember parts of the story that was so hard to accept. Sidney would console her, fortifying her through scripture.

Sidney was very much aware of Ryan's concern about the lack of relationship between his mother and grandfather. Over the past few years, Leslie's built up resentments, causing doubts, had subsided and the subject seldom came up, except when Ryan would go to the parole hearings for Nick. For days before the hearings, Leslie would not be herself until she learned of the outcome.

All of this was very much on his mind as he began to put his thoughts together. *"Father. Your grace surrounds me as I approach this subject. I'm aware that you have a purpose in putting this on my heart. Guide me, dear Lord, help me present this from your Word, as you intended it to be. I ask the Holy Spirit to prepare me for the prayer meeting so that those in attendance will understand the freeing power of forgiveness. In Jesus' Name. Amen."*

Leslie and Sidney welcomed each person as they came to their home for a prayer meeting. Soon the room was filled and Jeffrey said the opening prayer followed by the Lord's Prayer in unison.

In the middle of Sidney's lesson, he dilated the act of forgiveness, explaining that forgiveness is not a one-time thing. He told them, "The Bible teaches that even if someone sins against you seven times in a day but comes back seven times to you saying I repent you must forgive them. Just as through Christ, God forgives us, we also forgive." Then he continued. "In the Lord's Prayer, that we said together earlier, we ask that God forgive us our sins as we also forgive others for their sins. We are to be kind and compassionate to each other. We are to let go of all bitterness, rage, and anger, and all the resentment, and forgive each other, as the Lord has forgiven us."

Leslie sat quietly listening to every word. *How many times had Nick asked for her forgiveness?* She thought. *How many times had she forgiven him?* Maybe it was time, if not just for Ryan's sake, but for her own, it was time to forgive Nick, again. She realized he was much older now and she may run out of time.

The Cookbook

The revelation about Nick being her father happened when Ryan was young, not even five. All the years since still held hard feelings and sad memories. Since her mother died when Leslie was only eight years old, she had childlike memories of her. But, they were good memories until she was told about her father. Then there were more sad memories combined with the sad memories of losing her mother to pneumonia.

She knew Nick as a thief, part of a jewelry ring, that Sidney had been investigating. In her effort to find out Nick's background she unearthed some information that could have led to him being accused of murder. By setting the record straight, the truth revealed his identity as her father.

Later in another turn of events, Nick saved her little boy Ryan. So many things took place around the time when Nick was arrested and eventually put in prison, that lingered in the back of her mind for some fifteen years. This time in Leslie's life brought more grief as she began to question God. With the help of Sidney and Annabelle, her relationship with God became stronger than ever. Now she began to realize it was time to make amends and truly forgive Nick, for Ryan's sake.

Chapter 22

"I heard from the Sullies the other day," Leslie said as the Bordeaux and Rye family shared a meal at one of their favorite restaurants in the French Quarter, a little kid-friendly place that served hamburgers, onion rings with cheese sauce, and the girls favorite macaroni and cheese pizza.

"Who's that?" Jamie said wrinkling up her nose as she bit into a slice of pizza.

"The Sully's are good friends of ours who used to live in the French Quarter. They owned a drug store not far from here and Mr. Sully would prepare some of the best gumbo in town, in a crockpot in the back of the store, and the locals would come and get a bowl of it until it was all gone," Leslie told them. "And I now have Joe's recipe for my cookbook."

"Oh, I remember them," Karlah said. "Mom and I used to get there early before everyone else came."

"Do you remember that, Ryan?" Sidney said.

"I remember them, because Mr. Sully led our prayer meetings," Ryan said. "But I don't remember the gumbo part."

"They got us all started having prayer meetings. As Ryan said, Joe Sully conducted the prayer meetings like Sidney does now," Annabelle said.

"Where are they now?" Amy asked.

"Well, after Joe started having health problems they moved back to Dallas, Texas where they lived before coming to New Orleans. Karlah you must have been very young when you and your mother went to Sully's drug store," Leslie said.

"Well, I know I was young, maybe five or six when we first started going there, but I was still going there when I started school and on into middle school," Karlah said. "I think my mom knew them before I was born."

"Why wasn't I going there, mom?"

"Well, Ryan, we moved from the French Quarter before you were four so you probably don't remember going to the drug store," Leslie told him. "You and your mom remind me of me and my mom, Karlah. I was raised by a single mom and I never knew my father."

"What happened to your mom?" Karlah asked.

"She died when I was eight years old of pneumonia," Leslie told her.

Ryan listened to the conversation between his mom and Karlah hoping to understand more about his mom's childhood. It was interesting how much the two of them had in common.

"What happened to your father?" Karlah asked.

"I never knew him until Ryan was five."

The Cookbook

"Is he still alive?" Karlah asked.

"Yes, but he and I don't have a relationship. Ryan's grandfather is in jail," Leslie confessed as everyone at the table was waiting for Leslie to explain.

"I wish I had known my father. At least you know him, even if you're not close. I never met my father, and that haunts me sometimes. I wonder what kind of man he was. And, would he love me. You know what I mean?" Karlah said on the verge of tears. "I'm sorry."

"Don't be sorry, Karlah, it is quite understandable. I was like you for a long time, wondering about my father, who he was, was he still alive? My mother let me believe that he was out of the picture and I always believed he was dead. But, then I found out, and under unusual circumstances, that he had been alive all those years. But he hadn't known about me, either. We knew each other before we found out that he was my father," Leslie shared.

Annabelle looked at Sidney as tears came to her eyes. She wasn't sure if Leslie could continue but she knew how important it would be for Ryan, and it might help Karlah, also.

Jeffrey watched Karlah's pain and hoped somehow the dots would connect bringing her and Harry together. He had seen Leslie's pain when she found out that Nick was her father, and he didn't want that for Karlah and Harry.

"My mother told me that my father didn't know that she was pregnant because she found out the day he died. She had prepared a special dinner to celebrate. Then the police came to her door and told her my father had fallen off a roof at the construction site where he was working and died on the way to the hospital. The company compensated her, but it didn't last long, so she moved to a place called Barataria where her uncle lived. Do you know where that is?" Karlah asked.

Looking at Sidney, Leslie nodded her head. "Is that where you were born?" she asked.

"Yes."

"I didn't think there was a hospital in Barataria," Leslie stated.

"She had me at home with her aunt, who is a midwife, which was why she went there because she couldn't afford to go to a hospital."

"That was brave of her. I don't think I could do that," Annabelle said while Leslie got control of her emotions. Everyone at the table was quiet. Fortunately, the twins had gone to another table and were busy talking to friends, and hadn't heard the sad story.

"You said you found out about your father after Ryan was born. How did you find out? If you don't mind me asking."

Leslie looked at Ryan before she answered. "A woman I only knew as Mamma told me the whole story surrounding my mother's pregnancy."

Sidney took Leslie's hand in his and nodded encouraging her to continue.

"She told me that Nick, my father, had—as she put it—had his way with my mother, and he never knew she was pregnant and my mother never told anyone who the father was. You can imagine my horror at hearing this information from this stranger," Leslie said choking back the tears and looking at Ryan.

"Please, I'm so sorry I didn't mean to pry. How awful," Karlah said holding back her own tears.

The Cookbook

Ryan sat stunned. He had no idea, and felt ashamed that this had happened to his mother. What a horrible thing to be told, he thought. Now he knew why his mother couldn't be around Nick. He wanted to ask more questions but instead got up, and went to Leslie and put his arms around her.

"I love you, mom," he said kissing her cheek.

After he went back to his chair, Leslie answered Ryan's unasked question that she had forgiven Nick, but it was still very hard to accept him as her father.

Just then the twins came back to the table. Everyone put the conversation behind them and greeted the girls with smiles and small talk about their desserts. Karlah excused herself and headed to the lady's room. Leslie got up and followed her.

"You knew about all of this didn't you?" Ryan said to his father in a low accusing voice.

"Yes, but it was not my story to tell, son," Sidney clarified.

Then turning to Annabelle sitting next to him, he said. "That's what you meant about I would understand someday.

She nodded her head.

In the restroom Leslie put her arms around Karlah, hugging her she told her not to be upset. "Someday I was going to have to tell Ryan the truth and surrounded by people who care about him made it easier to share. So I don't want you to feel responsible in any way," she said backing up and looking her in the face. "Okay?"

"Okay," Karlah said wiping away her tears with her hands. "Actually, and don't take this wrong, I feel better knowing I'm not alone. Is that wrong?"

Molly Owen

"No. It's good to find out other people have a similar experience. We share something, you and I, that not many people share. And, Karlah, I believe God puts us with others who bare the pain of loss so they can support one another," Leslie said pulling a tissue from a box by the sink and handing it to her.

"Thank you, Leslie. You're a very kind person," Karlah said.

"Now, let's go join the others before they send someone in to check on us," Leslie said holding the door open and smiling at Karlah as she left the restroom ahead of her.

Ryan wanted to talk to his mother some more but he needed to take Karlah back to her dorm. So, he gave Lesley a hug and taking Karlah's arm the two of them said goodbye and left the restaurant.

Jeffrey announced that they needed to get the girls home and Annabelle stood up and went to Leslie.

"Are you alright?" she asked.

"Yes. Although this evening has raised some real questions, don't you think? Let's talk tomorrow," Lesley told her friend with a smile, letting her know she was okay.

*****

The next day found Leslie and Sidney full of unanswered questions brought on, not only by information from Karlah but, by many questions discussed after they arrived home the evening before. Sidney couldn't wait to hear from Charles who had come back to New Orleans the night before and Leslie couldn't wait to get to her laptop and follow up on Karlah's mom and the connection she had with the Sullies.

The Cookbook

Their morning devotional came from Romans, *"all things... work together for good."* They talked about how as believers they must not choose to become bitter. Not denying the pain of the unjust act against them, but as believers, they forgive the perpetrator and move on. Leslie knew only too well how hard this was, as her thoughts went to her son. Therefore, their prayer that morning was for Ryan's understanding and for Karlah to gain some peace.

Sidney filled his cup with coffee, for the second time, then with a cup in hand, he gave Leslie a kiss on the cheek and headed for the Studio. Leslie cleaned the breakfast dishes, dried her hands and went to her office where she opened her laptop in anticipation. Just then the phone rang.

"Good morning, Mrs. Bordeaux and how are you this bright sunshiny day?" Leslie said looking longingly at her computer.

"I'm doing fine. How are you? I thought after last night you may be in a down mood," Annabelle remarked.

"No. In fact, it is a load off my mind. I'm sure Ryan will be asking more questions but at least he knows why, now. What about Karlah? She shared some things last night that has put a whole new light on this Harry and Karlah thing, don't you think?"

"I just felt so sorry for her. Did she tell you any more when you two went to the Lady's room?" Annabelle asked.

"No. I just wanted to make sure she didn't take responsibility for what happened when I shared about Nick. She could see what it did to Ryan, and I didn't want her to be upset," Leslie said.

"I'm so glad you were able to talk about it. It'll be good to be able to have a conversation with Ryan. It will help him understand," Annabelle said with relief that it was out in the open.

"You know something else? I think it will help Ryan understand Karlah more too," Leslie said before telling Annabelle she needed to get busy, then saying goodbye.

*****

Ryan's mind was filled with questions, not only for his mother but his grandfather. Years of devotion between him and Nick, was now being challenged. The man he knew only as his grandfather, whom he loved and considered his friend, was now presented in a different light. For many years he wondered why his mother couldn't, or wouldn't, build a relationship with her father. Hearing Karlah's story about her father must have triggered his mother's own story. Clearly a hard subject for his mother, she presented it matter-of-factly, almost void of emotion. He was glad she had forgiven Nick, however, the pain of his actions seemed buried deep within her, hiding behind a curtain of shame, or was it disgust. Either way, Ryan wanted more of the story. He wanted to know this Mamma Leslie spoke of and how she knew so much about his grandfather.

Going about his morning routine, his thoughts went to the connection his mother and Karlah shared. At that moment, he realized that Karlah, like his mother, harbored unpleasant memories. It was beginning to make some sense concerning his feelings toward Karlah. Hearing her share her story with the people he loved and who loved him, brought the two of them to a more intimate place. On their ride back to Tulane, he approached the subject of Karlah's story with much hesitation. Karlah seemed more concerned about Ryan than herself. She kept apologizing for her role in Leslie's confession, knowing how painful it must have been for him.

"How sad to realize that a man you knew turns out to be your flesh and blood, a father you never knew. That would be hard to wrap your head around don't you think?" she said to Ryan.

"Yes. My mother's revelation has put me behind a rock and a hard place. I love my grandfather, but love and loyalty to my mother come first," Ryan confessed. "I just hope she can share the whole story with me someday."

Chapter **23**

Charles opened the door to the studio, walked to his desk, and laid his briefcase down, while Sidney waited patiently for the ritual to end. Charles went to the coffee pot and poured the last portion in his cup.

"So, how did it go? Did you find out anything that would shed some light on this case?" Sidney asked.

"Well, some of what I discovered didn't make a lot of sense."

"Like what?"

"Like the neighbor remembered the husband coming home and not finding his wife. She said he came over to her house and asked if she knew where Patricia was and she told him she had no idea. She went back to his house with him and there was no sign of someone giving birth. The neighbor said he insisted that his wife was in labor when she called him. Then he left for the closest hospital which was in Harvey. Later he came back and told her his wife wasn't there either," Charles said.

Sidney listened to what Charles told him but agreed it didn't make any sense. Then he told him what Karlah had shared at dinner the night before.

"So, who is the aunt and uncle her mother was staying with? Do you think Patricia could have gone there too?"

"Did the neighbor say anything about visitors to Harry's house that day?"

"As a matter of fact, she mentioned a lady she knew as a real estate agent had come by early that morning. But the neighbor left to run some errands and when she returned the lady's car was gone."

"Well, now we are getting somewhere. Could it have been Jennifer the neighbor saw?" Sidney said then picking up his cell, he called Leslie.

"I'll be right there," Leslie said picking up her laptop and cell phone and heading for the studio.

"Okay, let's put the information we now have together with the information we started with, and see if we can come up with a plan, now that we know that Karlah's mother had a midwife. This is the first time we've had a connection. We will need to track down Karlah's family history, like her mother's maiden name," Sidney said jotting down notes on a pad.

"Also, don't you think we should check on Jennifer's whereabouts around that time? Leslie asked.

"Right."

"Are you thinking that Jennifer had something to do with the babies?" Charles said to Leslie.

"Since she may have been seen the same day that Harry was unable to find his wife, I think it's highly possible, don't you?"

The Cookbook

Sidney agreed. "So Leslie, see what you can find out about Karlah's aunt and uncle, and we will get some background on Jennifer."

A plan in place, the investigative team got to work. Leslie was anxious to get started and began by researching Ben's sister Mary. She searched for a license for Mary Buck and found no one by that name on record going all the way to the time Karlah was born. Frustrated, she again looked for a birth certificate for Karlah. *Surely she has one?* She thought. *What if it's a fake?* Leslie was beginning to get worried, worried for Karlah. She searched until she finally came across a birth certificate under another name on the same day of birth, and with the right last name. It listed Karl Fetter as the father and Nancy Buck Fetter as the mother. The baby was named Nancy Karlah Fetter.

"That's it!" Leslie exclaimed.

Calling Sidney she told him the connection between Mary Buck and Karlah's mother. "Mary is indeed Karlah's mother's aunt. Her grandfather must be Samuel Buck, Ben's brother," she said. "Why haven't we heard about him?"

"Yes you would think she would have brought his name up at some point," Sidney said.

"Wait a minute," Leslie said looking at the screen on her laptop. "Samuel died. He died before Karlah was born. That's why she doesn't mention him, she never knew him," Leslie explained.

"Okay, now we're on the trail of something useful," Sidney said looking at Charles and giving a thumbs up. "At one point, didn't you tell me that the mother of a baby born at home would have to get a birth certificate from a doctor?"

"Yes," Leslie said thinking through the information she already knew. Her thoughts were twisting and turning like the Mississippi River that ran next to the French Quarter. With every turn of the story of not one but two babies capturing Leslie's attention. The thought still remained. *How did the babies get switched?* She studied the screen hoping she could willfully make the answer appear, but nothing happened.

It bothered her that Ben could be involved in this mystery. She thought back about her visit to his farm. She wondered as she remembered the farmhouse if that was where Karlah was born or was she born somewhere else and brought there? But, there would have to have been another baby. Perplexed, she began to think it was time for her to go back to Ben's farm. She knew it would be tricky since Sidney had already chastised her first visit there, but she had to get some answers, and at this point, the only way was to revisit Ben's farm and find out more about his sister Mary, the midwife.

Chapter **24**

For some time now, Karlah had wondered about her father's family and where she came from. Once again, she saw a commercial on TV about DNA testing. This time she was determined to send in for the kit, even if it would deplete her funds. The advertisement said the cost was discounted for only a short time. So writing a check she put it in an envelope with the information it asked for and, licking the flap, she closed the envelope, addressed, and stamped it. She would later put it in the mailbox outside her dorm.

*****

A few days later the kit came with instructions to spit in a container and send it back to the address in the box. Excitement filled her mind as she dropped the box with her sample in the same mailbox outside her dorm.

The next day she and Ryan made a picnic lunch from packaged sandwiches and bags of chips and containers of cut-

Molly Owen

up apples from the local store. They headed for Woldenberg Park on the riverfront to find a grassy place to sit and feel the breeze coming across the river, a welcome relief from the heat and humidity in the French Quarter surrounded by tall buildings and concrete sidewalks and crowded streets.

Ryan laid out a blanket borrowed from his mother and helped Karlah sit down with their food. He sat down beside her and put their study books on the blanket next to them. Quiet, except for a splash of water slapping against the walkway, they sat in silence looking out at the choppy water in the river as they ate their lunch.

"It sure is peaceful here," she said as a Frisbee came flying by missing her by inches. A young boy came running up to the blanket and, picking up the Frisbee, he apologized.

"Peaceful, you say," Ryan said laughing.

"Well, until the flying saucer almost hit me," she said laughing with him.

He gathered the remains of their picnic, jumped up, and headed for a trash container. When he came back, Karlah was lying down with her sunglasses shading her eyes. Her tanned body shown around her tank top and shorts. He sat back down on the blanket and laid next to her.

"When did you have time to get that great tan," he asked

"Actually it doesn't take much to darken this already darkened skin," she answered.

"I guess being out here in the sun shows it off," he said.

"I sent off a sample of my DNA today," Karlah said casually.

"Really? How does that work?"

The Cookbook

"They send you a kit, you spit in a tube and send it back to them. Then they test it and send you the results," she told him.

"So why did you do it?"

"I don't know much about my father's family, and I thought this would be a good way to find out about him," Karlah said turning toward him and leaning on her side.

"I see. That's interesting. Maybe I should do that so I can know more about my grandfather," Ryan said staring at the puffy white clouds hanging overhead. "Maybe that would tell me more about that Mamma character my mother talked about. The one that told her about her father."

"Yes, I remember. The place where you get the kit is having a sale now, if you are really interested," she told him laying back down.

"I'll think about it. I guess we better study before it gets too late."

"Ryan?"

"Yes," he said looking over at her.

"I hope you know that your mom and dad are very special," Karlah said.

"I do know that and I'm glad you see that too. They are very giving people and I hope that if you ever need them, you know that they will be there for you. For that matter, so will I, if the need ever arises."

"You must have forgotten, Ryan, you were there for me in the situation with Mr. Burke, remember?"

There was something about her that made him comfortable to be around her. They were getting to know each other better, and it felt right. He was glad that she liked his parents. He smiled, then opened his book and began to read. As if on cue, his cell phone rang. Looking at it he answered.

"Hi, Mom. What's up?"

"I thought you and Karlah could come over for dinner tomorrow night, if you aren't too busy with studies," Leslie said

"Hold on, I'll ask her. She's right here," Ryan said. Then turning to Karlah, "Mom wants us over for dinner tomorrow night. How about it?" he said.

"I think that'll work if we get back early," she said.

Leslie heard her and told Ryan they would make it an early meal. She was surprised and happy that they were spending more time together. She just didn't want it to get too serious. But then if it were God's plan she wouldn't interfere. She had an ulterior motive for inviting them to dinner. She hoped to be able to find out more about the circumstances surrounding Karlah's birth, and about her family, especially her mother's aunt Mary.

*****

"Hi, you two. Are you hungry?" Leslie said to Ryan and Karlah as they came through the backdoor into the kitchen.

"Sure does smell good. Whatever it is," Ryan said laughing at the family joke.

"They always laugh but they eat it all, so don't worry Karlah," Leslie said.

"It does smell good, what is it?" Karlah asked coming over to the stove.

"It's a Boudin. Have you ever had it?"

"It's like a sausage, isn't it? But, that looks like meatballs," Karlah said confused.

"Well, the sausage stuffing can be formed into meatballs instead of putting it into casings. So this recipe will be meatballs in a sauce served over rice," she told her.

"I can't wait to try it," she said following Ryan to the dining room where Sidney was setting the table. "Can we help?" she asked.

"Sure," Sidney said handing her a stack of napkins and Ryan the silverware.

Soon with the food ready and the table set, they all sat down for a meal together. Sidney asked Ryan to pray. *"Father, thank you for your grace through Jesus Christ our Lord and Savior. We ask your blessing on this food and on the one who prepared it. These things we ask in Jesus' Name. Amen."*

"Okay let's dig in, and see if this recipe will go in mom's cookbook," Ryan said giving Karlah a wink.

After many compliments to the cook, they finished their meal and waited for dessert. As Leslie passed the flan around the table, she told Karlah how she decided on what recipes to put in her cookbooks.

"Sidney and I went to the market one day after I started the garden and we came across a booth selling mirlitons. I was intrigued and began to talk to the seller. He invited me to his farm so he could show me how to grow them in my garden. His farm was in Barataria and his name was Ben, Ben Buck," Leslie said waiting for a reaction. "Later we saw him again at the market and met his sister Mary, who is a midwife," still no reaction Leslie asked. "I remember you said your mother went to her aunt to give birth because she was a midwife. If that is indeed your aunt, then that is quite a coincidence, isn't it."

"Did you go there?" Karlah asked

"Yes. It is a pretty place, well kept. As I said, I didn't meet Mary until later at the market."

"I've never been there. I really don't know much about them. My mother said she and her aunt had a falling out and she brought me with her back to the French Quarter. I never met them. Ben is my mother's uncle and his brother Samuel was my mother's father. He died before I was born." Karlah said. "They have never tried to contact me and I have no need to contact them."

"Do you know what the falling out was about?"

"Not really. That is about all I know about either side of my family. I told Ryan that I sent my DNA off, and I hope to find out more about my father's family. I almost feel like an orphan since I don't know anything about my ancestors."

Ryan noticed his mother's expression when she looked over at his father. He wondered if it had anything to do with Nick. It never occurred to him it may have something to do with Karlah.

"I was thinking about going back out there to ask Ben some more tips on gardening. He has quite a collection of native vegetables that I would like to try and grow. Would you like to go with me sometime?" Leslie asked.

Karlah sat quietly, then she looked at Ryan and asked him if he would go with them.

"Sure, I'll go, if that's alright with you, Mom?" Ryan said.

"Well, if it's going to be an outing then I'll go too," Sidney said winking at Leslie.

"Then it's set we'll all go," Leslie said laughing.

Karlah loved it when they all laughed, as she and Ryan did, over the simplest thing. She wasn't sure how simple this little trip to the Buck Farm would be. It may prove to be uncomfortable. But she was willing to go if it meant finding out more about her family and she was glad the Ryes would be going with her.

Chapter 25

The day arrived when Karlah was going to the Buck Farm with the Ryes. Ryan picked her up at her dorm and they headed for his folk's house. On the way, Karlah was quiet. Ryan asked if she was okay with the plan to go see her relatives.

"I don't know. It bothers me. Why didn't my mother make sure I knew her family? I think back about things she told me when I would ask questions. Now I don't think it made much sense. You know what I mean?"

"Actually, I do. I have always felt like something was missing in the story. Like it didn't all fit. When I would try to make it fit, I just got more confused," Ryan told her.

"Exactly, I've been thinking a lot about this ever since your mother suggested I go there. I don't know these people and they haven't made an effort over all these years to know me. Then I ask myself, why? Why didn't my mother make the effort for me to know them? She told me stories when she was growing up,

Molly Owen

and how she spent time on the farm, and how much she loved it. As I was growing up, you would have thought she would have wanted me to have those same experiences. She talked about her father, Samuel, all the time, but never about his brother and sister. What happened to make her turn against them? It all happened after I was born. I don't know Ryan, I'm not sure I want to know what happened," Karlah said staring out the side window of the truck.

"I understand and Karlah you don't have to go if you don't want too. I'm sure mom would understand," Ryan assured her.

"No. I need to go. Maybe I can get some answers to a few of my questions. Let's just go and see what happens. I may not find out anything anyway," she told him as they pulled into the driveway.

Leslie had packed a picnic lunch for all of them, and Sidney put the basket in the trunk of his car while the other three got in and shut the doors. Leslie looked back at Ryan and Karlah and told them about the plans for lunch.

"I thought it would be fun to have a picnic at a little park I saw on the way to your uncle's farm," she said.

"Sounds great, mom," Ryan said taking Karlah's hand and giving it a squeeze.

Sidney pulled off the road and drove to a spot under a tree and parked. "How's this?" he said looking over at Leslie.

"Perfect," she said getting out of the car.

Ryan and Karlah helped her spread a blanket on the ground. Sidney brought the basket of food and set it down in the middle. They gathered around sitting next to each other. There was a slight breeze keeping the heat index down. As Leslie passed out plates and food, the conversation went to the Buck Farm.

The Cookbook

"I'm surprised you haven't spent any time on your uncle's farm. It is quite large and as a child, it would have been a lot of fun," Leslie said hoping to spark a memory from Karlah.

"I was just telling Ryan earlier that I was surprised that my mom didn't bring me to the farm. She always talked about how much fun she had there growing up," Karlah said. "There seems to be some holes in my past that hopefully my aunt and uncle can fill in for me."

"Maybe they can," she said looking at Sidney.

After cleaning up the area and putting the blanket and basket back in the car, they headed down the road toward Barataria. Coming to Buck Farm Lane, Sidney turned and followed along a field of crops ready for picking. The smell of freshly mowed grass filled their nostrils as they came upon the farmhouse and barn. Sidney maneuvered the car into a parking spot off the driveway and stopped the car as Ben came out of the barn and walked toward them.

"Hi, Ben, you remember my husband Sidney. And this is our son Ryan and friend Karlah," Leslie said introducing the group. "We came to see how your mirlitons are doing and see if there is any other plant I may be interested in."

"Well, you have come at the right time. The mirlitons are ripe for the picking and I may have some other plants you may want for your garden," Ben said without missing a beat. It was obvious he didn't recognize Karlah as they followed him around the barn and into the garden. There they found Mary, bent over pulling weeds.

"Mary, you remember Leslie and her husband. This is their son and friend. Sorry, can't remember your name," Ben said as Mary stood up and offered her hand to Leslie, after removing her gloves.

"Yes, I remember. We met at the market," she said shaking Leslie's hand. Then she looked at Ryan and Karlah. "Nice to have young people.. We don't get to see many youngsters out here anymore."

"My mother used to tell me stories about coming out here," Karlah said.

"Really, who was your mother?" Ben said.

"Nancy, Nancy Fetter. My grandfather was Samuel Buck," Karlah said hoping for recognition.

Leslie watched Mary as her face went ashen and she started to shake. "Are you alright, Mary," she asked.

"She's fine. Just too much sun. You better go inside and cool off," Ben told his sister.

"We'll help her, mom, you go ahead and talk to Mr. Ben," Ryan said helping Mary toward the house with Karlah close behind.

They went through the kitchen door and Mary sat down at the table with Karlah sitting across from her. Ryan got a glass and filled it with water from the faucet and offered it to Mary.

"Thank you, son," she said.

"Can you tell me about my mother?" Karlah asked.

"What do you want to know?" Mary said.

"What was the disagreement that kept my mother from coming back here? Did you help deliver me?"

Mary took another sip of water and put the glass on the table. Just then, Leslie, Ben, and Sidney came through the kitchen door and stood behind Mary facing Karlah.

The Cookbook

"Yes, I helped your mother deliver," Mary said. "It was hard labor. It took several hours. Then that real estate lady brought me another woman in labor so I was going back and forth between them."

Leslie nudged Sidney. "Do you remember the real estate lady's name? Was it Jennifer?" he asked.

"That sounds right. This other lady was in real trouble. It was her first and a big baby. After the birth, I couldn't stop the bleeding. I called for an ambulance but she died before they got here. The ambulance took the mother and baby straight to the funeral home." Mary said.

"They both died?" Leslie asked.

"But, what about my mother?" Karlah said before Mary could answer Leslie's question.

"Your mother came out here to deliver her baby. But she went into labor at 32 weeks. She had just lost her husband and that had caused her a lot of stress. She didn't eat right or take care of herself while she was pregnant and now she was about to lose her baby," Mary said.

Mary's heart was pounding out of her chest as she remembered the events of that day twenty-some years earlier. She had held this secret close to her all these years. Now she knew to reveal the truth of that day could cause her a lot of trouble. But she wanted to clear her conscience and this child sitting across from her should know the truth. She clasped her hands together and laid them in her lap. And looking up at Ben, who had moved to the corner in front of her, she took a deep breath.

"I felt so sorry for Nancy and didn't want her to suffer more loss and that real estate lady encouraged me to switch the

Molly Owen

babies. She told me that the live baby didn't have a mother and the stillborn baby didn't need a mother. So I took the live baby and gave it to Nancy. Then I sent the baby that Nancy gave birth to with the women that died.

Nancy stayed with us for almost a year, but she became suspicious because you had no resemblance to her husband or herself—hair, eyes, darker complexion, even your facial features—and she was very surprised at how big you were at birth. You see, she had only gained about 8 pounds and you weighed over nine pounds at birth. She kept asking me how this was all possible. So finally, I told her the truth. She became very angry. Then one night she packed her bags, and after telling me she hated me, and she never wanted to see me again, she left," Mary finished with her head held down, eyes looking at her hands in her lap.

The room was deadly quiet. No one said a word. Karlah sat stunned. She didn't move, she just stared at Mary in disbelief. Ryan put his hand on her shoulder, and she still didn't move. *How do I process this?* She asked herself. Thoughts swirled around in her brain trying to put some sense to what she had just heard. Slowly she got up from her chair and walked toward the kitchen door. Pushing it open she walk out toward the garden.

Ryan started to go after her but Leslie told him that she would go after her. She followed Karlah until they were both standing in the garden.

"How could she? Why didn't she tell me? My whole life has been a lie. Maybe her story about my father was also a lie. My father? Oh no. Who is my father?" Karlah began to cry.

"I'm so sorry, Karlah, I understand that this is quite a shock. But you are not alone. We are right beside you and we will be there whenever you need us," Leslie said holding her in her arms.

"I don't know what to do, Leslie. How did you handle it?" Karlah said tears covering her face.

"I handled it very poorly until I realized that Jesus was my salvation and he would be there for me. Sidney and Annabelle were my support as I reclaimed myself. Karlah, it is easy to get lost in your hurt and the sorrow of lost time in your past. But, if you work hard to forgive and move forward it will give you peace. There is a verse in the Bible that stays with me daily. *Proverbs 3:5, Trust in the Lord with all your heart, do not depend on your own understanding.* Memorize that scripture and depend on God to see you through. There are many things that happen to us throughout our lives that we do not understand. If we trust in the Lord we will be able to forgive those who have harmed us and we will grow from the experience. God loves you, Karlah, and he is in your corner." Leslie said.

"And, Karlah, we will be there to support you," Ryan said. "You have the whole Rye clan with you now and we'll see you through this, I promise."

Karlah dried her tears and gave Leslie a hug. She looked at Ryan and smiled. He went to her and put his arms around her and held her until she relaxed and stepped back from him. Surrounded by her newfound family she let her anger and fear leave for the time being.

"I need to say goodbye to Ben…" hesitating "and Mary," Karlah said walking back toward the house.

Mary still sat at the table where Karlah left her. Sitting down across from her, Karlah put her hand out across the table. Mary looked at her then reached for her hand. They looked at each other with deep emotion, neither saying a word. Ben watched from the corner of the kitchen. Finally, Karlah spoke.

"I don't condone what you did, Mary, but I think your heart was in the right place. It will take some time for me to process everything. I hope I'll come to the point where I can forgive you and my…Nancy for keeping me from my true family. For now, I will say goodbye to you both. We will probably not be seeing each other again," she said, getting up and walking out the door.

Chapter *26*

Convinced, by Jennifer, to go to the prayer meeting at the Ryes, the three of them prepared to go together. Sarah was elated, not only that both her parents were going with her, but that she would be with her friends. Jennifer was excited because she would be in the same circle as her idol, Annabelle. Harry wasn't sure how he felt at this point. He was fully aware of Jennifer's motives but was glad they were together for Sarah's sake.

Jennifer demanded that they arrive late so they could make a grand entrance. As they arrived at the Ryes, Harry automatically drove around back to park, however, the area was already full of cars. Jennifer was so involved in her own desires that she didn't question how Harry knew to go to the back to park. He drove past the Studio and went around to the front. He stopped and let Sarah and Jennifer out.

"I'll go find a place to park, don't wait for me, and go on in. I'll be there shortly," Harry said.

Jennifer pushed Sarah in front of her as the door opened to let them inside. They were greeted by Ryan. As they entered the room, she looked around as many familiar faces turned to greet them. Ryan brought in a couple more chairs, and Sarah told him her father was parking the car and would need a chair too. Ryan looked over at Karlah. But, she hadn't heard the conversation. Just then the door opened and Ryan put another chair next to Sarah for Harry then went and sat down next to Karlah.

Jeffrey noticed the newcomers and started the meeting with a prayer. *"Most Heavenly Father, You are an awesome God, King of Kings and Lord of all. We thank you for the blessings you bestow on us daily. We thank you for your grace, for our savior Jesus Christ who died on the cross for our sins. We ask your blessing on each and every one among us today. And Lord, if anyone present today is harboring guilt and needs forgiveness we pray they will come to you. We love you, and we thank you for loving us. We pray this in the name of Jesus Christ our Lord. Amen."*

Annabelle and Jeffrey were aware of the events that took place in Barataria the day before. So, to see the Burke family at the meeting brought many questions to mind. Not only because of the issue around Harry and Karlah, but why was Jennifer with them? Could it be that she was ready to clear her conscious? Annabelle took Jeffrey's hand when he sat down to acknowledge their thoughts were on the same wavelength.

As the opening prayer ended, it was time for the young people to leave for their meeting. Ryan and Karlah stood up and motioned for the others to follow them. The twins saw Sarah and told her to come upstairs with them. Sarah looked at her father for permission then went with them. On her way, she caught up with Karlah and gave her a big hug.

The Cookbook

Harry was surprised and delighted as his heart skipped a beat when he walked into the room and saw Karlah at the meeting. He hadn't seen her for several weeks and to see her now out of the gym brought him such joy. Her hair pulled back in a bun at the nape of her neck was the very way his wife, Patricia, wore her hair sometimes.

He sat, star-struck, watching Karlah and Sarah hugging each other as they left the room. *They could be sisters.* He thought. If only Sidney could figure out the mystery behind his innate feeling that Karlah was his daughter.

Sidney stood up and walked to the front of the group. He greeted everyone and thanked them for coming. As he scanned the room he saw Ryan holding Karlah's hand as they gathered the young people to go upstairs. He wondered if she had seen Harry come into the room. He started his talk by asking the question.

"Have you taken Jesus as your Savior? When this life on earth is over, do you know where you will be? As sinners, we know that only through Jesus Christ will our sins be forgiven. God sent his only son to die for us on the cross to give us everlasting life with him. As believers, we receive His grace when we confess our sins and ask forgiveness. God watches over us and knows our deepest thoughts. Our Lord is the only one who will judge our sins. Our Father in heaven waits for us to bring our earthly troubles to him. If anyone here today needs to lift a burden from their shoulders, please take it to the Lord. I'll be here after the meeting to help anyone through prayer," Sidney said and closed with the Lord's Prayer in unison.

After the prayer meeting, everyone in the group stood up and began to greet each other. Some of the women went to the kitchen to lay out the food for the potluck lunch. Others gather around in small groups for conversation. As Annabelle headed for the kitchen, Jennifer walked up to her and started asking her questions.

Jennifer was almost giddy as she began to engage Annabelle in conversation. She knew she was overacting, but couldn't stop herself. Annabelle, in her eyes, was everything she could hope to be. She was beautiful, educated, and married to a man that was once the most eligible bachelor in New Orleans. She was very articulate, and so refined in her mannerisms.

Leslie soon came over to rescue Annabelle and introduced herself. "Hello, I'm Leslie Rye, and you must be Jennifer, Harry's wife. We love having you and your family here today," she said a little ashamed of herself for the true feelings she had. She was glad to see Harry and Sarah but now had reservations about Jennifer. *"Forgive me, Father, I am not her judge."* She prayed.

"I told Harry that we really needed, for Sarah's sake, to find a place to worship God," Jennifer said in all sincerity.

"Well, come join us for a potluck lunch," Leslie said noticing that Sidney was headed towards Harry.

"Hello, Harry. Glad to see you here this morning," Sidney said offering his hand for a shake.

"Thank you. I appreciated your talk. This was Jennifer's idea, well, actually Sarah and Jennifer thought it was a good idea, but I'm glad we came," he said. Then looking around to see if anyone was listening he asked if Sidney was making progress on the investigation.

"As a matter of fact, we may be getting somewhere. Why don't you come to see me tomorrow?" Sidney told him.

Karlah was surprised to see Sarah at the meeting with both of her parents. However, she was glad to be there. After the

The Cookbook

emotional day the day before, she didn't dwell on issues with Sarah's father. When the young people came back after their meeting to rejoin the group, Ryan stood close by Karlah to help avoid any awkwardness if Harry approached them. He saw his dad talking to Harry and wondered if they were talking about Karlah.

After everyone left, Ryan took Karlah back to her dorm. She hadn't been to her mailbox in a few days and stopped there to see if she had anything. Thumbing through several pieces of mail she noticed one from the DNA Company where she had sent in her sample. Carefully opening the envelope, she pulled out a piece of paper that told her the origin of her ancestors. A letter with the test results said to go to their web site and start a family tree. *How am I going to do that, when I don't know anything beyond my own name? And even that was wrong* she thought with a big sigh. Walking into her dorm room, she laid the mail on the table determined to check on it later.

*****

Meanwhile, as she and Sidney finished putting things away after the prayer meeting, Leslie decided to confide in Sidney. She had been doing some soul searching and shared with him, her desire to go see Nick.

"All of this revelation with Karlah's father has made me realize that I need to forgive Nick again. Your lesson on forgiveness gave me food for thought. And, Sid, if I am going to be able to help Karlah, I need to do the same thing I want for her to do. Forgiveness will set us both free. I know I told Nick years ago I forgave him. But I don't think I really did. I have carried all this anger in my heart for years. It's time to let go and truly forgive him," Leslie confessed.

"I'm proud of you, Leslie, I think you are ready. I think you are right about sharing your forgiveness of Nick with Karlah. If what we think is true, she will need help forgiving the people who have hurt her. It looks like Jennifer had something to do with all of this and that will hurt Harry even more. I talked to Harry this morning and he is coming to our office in the morning. I want to tell him what we found out yesterday at the Buck Farm."

"Even the part about Jennifer?" Leslie said concerned.

"I don't know. What do you think?"

"I just find it strange, first of all, that Jennifer doesn't see the resemblance of Karlah and her birth mother, who was supposedly her friend, and second, don't you find it coincidental that the three of them came to prayer meeting?"

"Yeah, Harry said it was her idea to come," Sidney said with a puzzled look on his face. "Do you think either one of them realized that Karlah would be there?"

"I really don't know but I think we had better put this in God's hands. We are involved in some really deep emotions that could cause some real problems, Sidney," Leslie said very concernedly.

Sidney took Leslie's hands in his as he began to pray. *"Father, Leslie is right. We are about to reveal some long-held secrets that could cause more hurt than the parties involved may be able to handle. We ask your guidance as we go forward. Give us the words and the ability to present this revelation in a kind, compassionate manner. Help us to be there for the people involved. I think about sweet Sarah and what this may do to her, Lord. Please keep us in your sight as we proceed. We ask this in Jesus' Name. Amen."*

The Cookbook

Chapter **27**

Harry's anxiety increased the closer he came to Sidney's office. His thoughts scrambled as he went back and forth between wanting his suspicion to be true, knowing what that would do to his family, and if it wasn't true, let go of his desire to have Karlah be his daughter. Daily, he found himself staring at Sarah and seeing the resemblance in her. It was the same things he saw in Karlah, a part of himself. *Oh, Lord, I need answers. I can't move forward until I know. Please, Lord, I need peace with this. Be with me as I hear what Sidney has to tell me. Amen.* Harry said, realizing that it was the first prayer he had said since the day he drove like crazy to get to his wife before their baby was born. He remembered now how he had prayed over and over, only to find out his world was, as he knew it, gone forever.

He pulled into the parking space and sat a minute before shutting the ignition off. *This is it. Good or bad. Real or unreal, I have to know.* He thought as he slowly got out of the car and walked to the door in the studio. Inside he found Sidney, Leslie, Jeffrey and Annabelle.

"Good morning Harry. Come on in and have a seat. I know you are wondering why I have everyone here. After I share with you, I want you to know we all support you, and we will be here if and when you need us."

Harry sat down as he felt his heart pounding and his breathing labored. Before he could say anything, Sidney asked if they could pray.

Taking each other's hands Sidney began to ask their heavenly father to be with them. *"Father, we give this matter to you. We ask your blessing on Harry as he hears this news. Give him strength and courage, Father. And give me the right words, Lord Jesus. In Your Name. Amen."*

It was short and to the point as Harry braced himself for what was to come. At first, when Sidney spoke, Harry couldn't focus on what he was saying. Something about a farm. His brain was questioning everything as if it were a trial. Then Sidney began to tell him about Mary's confession to Karlah. As the shock set in Harry wasn't aware that tears were pouring down his face. He sat stunned trying to absorb the information. His thoughts went to his beloved wife. The agony she must have felt, all alone, without him there to hold her, protect her, even to say goodbye. He wondered if she was able to see her baby, hold her. Unaware of the people around him, he lowered his head and pulled in his shoulders, and leaning toward his lap, he began to sob. At the time of her death, he went through the motions of making arrangements and keeping himself brave, almost stoic. But now all the pent up emotion was let out and he was afraid it may not stop.

The Cookbook

Leslie, with tears in her eyes, went to him. She handed him a box of tissues, and pulled her chair over next to him. He looked at her in disbelief. He had only heard the part about the woman who died and was buried with someone else's baby. Now he was processing the rest of the story. His baby was alive. He raised his head, and looked at Sidney.

"The baby?" he asked.

"All indications are that Karlah is your daughter. We will need proof, but that will be easy enough to get. Karlah sent off for her DNA test a while back not knowing it would help prove that you are her father. She is very upset by all this, as you can imagine," Sidney told him.

"Does she suspect anything? That I'm her father?" Harry questioned.

"Not at all. Why would she?" Sidney said. "We have not said anything to her or to Ryan for that matter."

"I don't understand. How did you know about this midwife?" Harry asked becoming more himself.

"That's a long story. Leslie is the one who put it together after hearing Karlah's story about her mother and her mother's aunt," he said.

"Her mother? What do you mean?"

"She knows now that Nancy wasn't her mother," Leslie told him. "But she doesn't know who her real parents are. I'm sure as she is able to put things together, she is going to want to know, and will start searching. Right now she is still in shock, just like you are. After you process the information we have given you, it will be up to you to decide when to tell Karlah. It doesn't have to be right away. You have other things to deal with now."

"Yes. What to tell my family?"

Sidney decided not to reveal any more information at this time after seeing how it had affected Harry. It would be interesting, however, to hear Jennifer's reaction to the news.

"Since all of you are aware of everything, it might be a good idea for me to tell Jennifer with you present," Harry said.

Sidney looked at Leslie, then at Annabelle and Jeffrey. "We are willing to do that, if that is what you want," Sidney told him. "Do you want to tell Karlah before you tell your family?"

Chapter 28

The decision was made to have Karlah and Ryan over as soon as possible depending on their class schedules.

"What do you think this is about?" Karlah asked on the way to Ryan's parents.

"I have no idea," Ryan said puzzled at the urgency in his mom's voice when she called and insisted he and Karlah come together to their home that afternoon.

"Do you think it could be about my father?" Karlah said hopefully.

"I think she would have said something if that were the case, don't you?" Ryan said.

"I guess so. I guess I was just hoping. Did I tell you about the mail I got from the DNA place?"

"Yes. Have you thought any more about that? You know, doing your family tree," Ryan asked turning into the driveway next to another unfamiliar car parked in the back.

"I guess all they really need is my DNA to start the family tree. I don't know Ryan, it is still kind of scary," Karlah said looking over at him.

"Well, let's go see what this is all about, shall we," he said getting out of the truck and going around to open her door.

He opened the back door to the kitchen and let Karlah go ahead of him. They walked into the kitchen where Leslie was waiting for them. She offered them a glass of iced tea and handing each a full glass then she led the way to the dining room. Harry had his back to them with Sidney sitting facing them. At first, they didn't recognize Harry. But then he stood up and turned around.

"Hello, Karlah, you must be Ryan, pleased to meet you," Harry said offering his hand as Ryan shook it and pulled out a chair for Karlah. "How are your classes going?" Harry said to Karlah, who answered, "Okay," wondering what was going on.

"Karlah, we have something to share with you. We know you had a real shock last Saturday at the Buck Farm and after we did some investigating we have discovered some more information involving Mr... Harry," Sidney stated. "Before we go any further I want you to know that the information has not been legally verified. However, we are certain that it can easily be proven."

Karlah began to shake. She stared at Harry who smiled at her with tears in his eyes. Before anyone could say anything else, Karlah, taking Ryan's hand, slowly formed the words... "Are you my father?"

The Cookbook

"Yes," Harry, with tears pushing passed his eyelids, said nodding his head.

Everyone sat quietly as the words hung in the air. Ryan still holding her hand, was not sure what to do. *This is the man that Karlah had been afraid of, and now he's saying he's her father. How could that be?* He thought. Then, as if an answer to his unasked question. Harry began to tell the story of how he was taken aback by Karlah at the gym. She was a carbon copy of her mother, and that is why he couldn't take his eyes off her.

"I know now what you must have thought of me at the time, Karlah, but you look like I remember your mother looked at about the age you are now. You even wear your hair the same way sometimes, back in a bun, as she wore hers. I'm sorry if I frighten you. That was not my intention at all. It wasn't until Jeffrey... Mr. Bordeaux told me how upset you were that I knew I had to get help to find out if you were indeed my daughter. That's when I hired Ryan's father to investigate. So, this morning he told me about your encounter with the midwife and the story she told you. It all started to make sense. I wasn't there when you were born. Patricia, that was your mother's name, called me and she was in labor. I was out of town and I tried to get there. But I was too late... please don't cry." Harry said reaching for Karlah's hand.

Ryan let go of her hand and moved out of the way as Karlah and Harry stood up and embraced, holding each other tightly both crying tears of hurt and joy all at the same time. Karlah reached for the tissues on the table and sat back down. Harry sat down beside her.

"Does that mean that Sarah is my little sister?" Karlah said with a smile as she wiped away the tears on her face.

"It does. And I'm sure she will be thrilled," he said nodding his head.

As everyone began to absorb the information they had just received, Sidney asked to say a prayer. *"Heavenly Father, we gather here today in your presence as we share together the reunion of two people: father, and daughter. We ask that you bless this time with them as they build a new relationship. Give them the strength and courage as they put their faith in you. Help them to put the past behind them as they embrace the future. Father, be with those close to Karlah and Harry as they support them through love, patience, and guidance through your holy Word. Lord, we thank you for so many blessings here today. And Lord Jesus, help us share our remembered past struggles and how we overcame them with your help. You are our King of Kings and we put our trust in you. In Jesus' Holy Name, we pray. Amen."*

"Thank you," Harry and Karlah said in unison then smiled at each other.

"I really do need to get back for my next class, but I want to hear all about my mother," Karlah said. *My mother, my real mother, Patricia,* she thought.

"Yes, me too," Ryan said standing up as Harry stood up and shook his hand.

"I will be in touch soon, Karlah, so we can get together again. I don't want to keep you young people, away from your studies," Harry said giving her a hug.

After Karlah and Ryan left Harry sat involved in his own thoughts. He was glad things went so well. He was fully aware that the next hurdle may not be as easy. The thought of telling Jennifer he had another daughter scared him. Knowing how she felt about having one child he knew two children would be way beyond her comfort zone. Of course, she wouldn't have to deal with Karlah except when the sisters wanted to be together. *Sisters? How wonderful for both of them.* He thought. To have a complete family unit was a pipe dream. He knew Jennifer would never agree to that. Knowing Jennifer as he did, he was well aware of her lack of motherly traits. Blessed by his daughter Sarah, which in itself was just short of a miracle since Jennifer never wanted children, he would protect her at all costs.

Leslie poured Sidney and Harry another cup of coffee, then sat down at the table. "Do you still want everyone there when you tell Jennifer?"

"Yes, I think it will be easier. She may not take this well. I'm really surprised that she didn't see the resemblance as I did. After all, she was Patricia's friend and she spent a lot of time with her and me for that matter. She was a big help for me after Patricia and the baby died, and she helped me sell the agency. We aren't exactly a marriage made in heaven, but it produced Sarah, and I'm very grateful for that," then taking a breath, "When would it be convenient for the four of you?" he asked.

"How about tonight? Come for supper. You can bring Sarah and the Bordeauxs can bring the girls. They can go upstairs while we talk," Sidney said.

"If that works for everyone else, then I will check with Jennifer," Harry said, thanking them for all their kindness.

Jennifer could hardly contain herself when Harry called her to let her know that they had been invited for a meal at the Rye's and that Annabelle would be there, also.

"Of course we can make it. Silly, this is a dream come true," she said not questioning it for a moment.

Molly Owen

Harry's heart began to pound again thinking about what was ahead. He knew Jennifer's desire to be part of the upper-class in New Orleans and this, she thought, was just the beginning. It concerned him that Sarah would be there, not knowing how Jennifer would react to the news. His hope was that she would accept it and welcome Karlah into their world. For Sarah and Karlah's sakes, he wanted Jennifer to treat it with respect. For some reason, his thought was dwelling on the past. He was thinking back about the time around Patricia's death. He remembered Jennifer coming to him at the funeral home. He couldn't remember how she knew what had happened. She just showed up and basically took over. At the time he was very grateful. But, looking back he now realized that there were things he didn't remember, that he should have remembered. He was always grateful for Jennifer's help and her concern for him as he went through his grieving. But things had changed and he wondered… no, he wouldn't go there. Not now that he had Karlah back.

Meanwhile, Sidney had gone out to his office while Harry called Jennifer. In a few minutes, Harry knocked on the office door.

"Just want to thank you again for all you have done. I think it went well with Karlah. I don't think it will go as well with Jennifer," Harry said before leaving.

Leslie called Annabelle to talk about the events earlier in the day. She told her how proud she was of Karlah. "She took it very well, better than I did finding out who my father was, speaking of which I have decided to go see Nick,"

"Really? What brought that on?" Annabelle said loudly as to be heard in the speaker on her cell phone while gathering the papers from her desk and putting them into her briefcase.

The Cookbook

"I just want to be a role model for Karlah… and Ryan," she said.

"Have you told Ryan?"

"Not yet, I'll let things die down a little bit first."

"Do you want me to bring anything tonight?" she asked Leslie.

"No. I've got it. Just come and get ready for a show because Sidney didn't tell Harry about the role Jennifer played in the baby swap so it should be interesting,"

"Do you think that is wise? Blindsiding Harry?" Annabelle questioned.

"I think Sidney wants to see her reaction when Harry reveals Karlah's true identity," Leslie tells her. "I'm glad you will be there, for legal counsel if needed."

"Well, we will see you later and I pray all goes well for Sarah's sake," Annabelle said before hanging up.

*****

The ride back to the dorm was filled with silence, then laughter, then tears as Karlah absorbed everything.

"Thank you, God." She said over and over again. "Thank you that Mr. …no, my father is a good man," Karlah said turning to look at Ryan.

"I don't know about you, but I'm still in shock," Ryan said smiling back.

"I can't believe this is happening. I not only have a father but a sister. Can you believe it, Ryan?" Karlah said then shaking her head she began to cry.

Ryan pulled into a parking space close to the building where Karlah had her next class. Turning off the ignition he turned and took her in his arms. Holding her until she stopped crying.

As he let her go he said. "It's okay. Are you sure you want to go to class?"

"No. But I can't afford to miss this class. He's going to give a major test next week. I don't know if I can concentrate, but I have to try and I'll need to really study," she said looking at Ryan for support.

"You can do this Karlah. I'm sure this will be hard, but try to put things behind you and don't forget that God can help. Just talk to Him. He'll give you strength as you need it. I'll help in any way I can. I love you, Karlah. I'm proud of you. You are going to be just fine," he said taking her in his arms again, and hugging her.

"Ryan?" She said

"Yes."

"I love you too. I have for a while now,"

"Me too," he said smiling.

Chapter **29**

"Hurry up, Sarah, we don't want to keep the Rye's waiting," Jennifer yelled down the hall to Sarah's room. Jennifer's excitement level was at a peak as she made sure her outfit fit the occasion.

"You look very nice," Harry said noticing her anxiety.

"You think so? I'm not overdressed am I?" she said looking at herself, one more time, in the full-length mirror.

"No. You look just fine," he said as Sarah came down the hall and took his hand.

They arrived at the same time as the Bordeaux family. The girls began to giggle as they went ahead of the adults and up the backstairs into the kitchen. They took turns hugging Leslie then went upstairs to the den.

Jennifer and Annabelle went ahead of Jeffrey with Harry being the last one through the door, then as he shut it, he sighed

Molly Owen

and took a cleansing breath before he entered the kitchen where everyone was greeting Leslie and Sidney.

"Supper is almost ready. So let's find a seat at the table. Sidney will you call the girls down so we can eat. There is room at the table for them to sit with us," Leslie said taking the Gumbo off the stove. "Nothing fancy. We're having shrimp gumbo and bread pudding for dessert."

"Well, it sure does smell good," Harry said pulling out a chair for Jennifer then sitting down beside her.

After the girls were seated, Sidney said grace. *"Thank you, Father, for this food and for Leslie who prepared it and thanks to you for our company as they share it with us. In Jesus' name. Amen."*

There was chatter from the girls throughout the meal. Even though it was uncomfortable at times everyone managed to keep the conversation going. Sidney helped Leslie clear the gumbo bowls and put out the pudding for dessert. Leslie told the girls they could take their dessert upstairs then she poured everyone a cup of coffee.

"This is really good, Leslie," Jennifer said taking a bite. "You're a very good cook."

"Thank you, Jennifer, I'm glad you like it," Leslie said.

Soon the desserts were finished and the table cleared. Everyone went to the living room where each one found a seat. Harry sat next to Jennifer and clearing his throat he looked over at her.

"Jennifer, I have something to tell you, and since the Ryes and Bordeauxs have been a part of this discovery, I thought it would be best if they were here when I told you," Harry said.

The Cookbook

"Told me what, Harry?" Jennifer looked puzzled. *Now, what is he up to? This evening was going so well. Please don't spoil it.* She thought.

"It's about Karlah,"

"Karlah? The gymnastics instructor? What about her?"

"For some time now I have noticed how much she reminds me of Patricia," he said.

"Patricia?" Jennifer said shaking her head. "What are you saying?"

"I now have proof, with the help of Sidney, that Karlah is my daughter," he said bracing for her reaction.

"Your daughter?" Jennifer said as her heart felt like it had stopped beating.

Leslie thought an explanation was in order. "You see, Nancy, the only mother Karlah knew gave birth with a midwife who was her aunt. We figured out who her aunt was, and last Saturday we went to see her at the Buck Farm in Barataria, you know, where Harry and Patricia lived. The aunt told Karlah about two women giving birth at the same time and how she switched the babies," she said looking right at Jennifer.

Jennifer's face went pale and her breathing became labored. "So what are you saying? I don't understand," she said trying to think.

"Nancy gave birth to a stillborn and Patricia gave birth to Karlah, but Patricia died before the midwife could save her. She told us how Nancy, her niece, had lost her husband and she felt sorry for her and with the encouragement of a real estate lady she gave Karlah to her niece and sent Nancy's deceased baby with Patricia's body when the ambulance came."

Molly Owen

There was a hush over the room as everyone waited for all the information to sink in. Harry looked at Jennifer in disbelief.

"You were there," Harry said to her as he absorbed what Leslie had just said.

"Harry, you don't understand," Jennifer said with tears in her eyes. "It was better that way, better for you. You couldn't raise a child on your own."

"You knew all along… how could you? You never wanted children. I had to beg you to have Sarah. You didn't want Karlah, either. You just wanted to be married to me. Isn't that right?" Harry said moving away from her.

"Let's keep our voices down, we don't want the girls to hear what's going on," Sidney said. "Harry, don't you and Jennifer want to go out to my office to finish this conversation? I'll go with you."

Harry stood up and told her to come with him. Jennifer pulled back but Harry looked at her sternly and motioned for her to come. She walked in front of him through the kitchen and out the back door to the studio in the back.

Sidney went ahead of them and unlocked the door. Once inside the three of them sat down. Harry, still angry, looked at Jennifer, who hung her head down and didn't look up at him. Silence filled the room. Finally, Jennifer spoke.

"Harry, I know what we did was not right, but our intentions were good. Mary the midwife was concerned about her niece. She was afraid if she knew her baby had died it would contribute to the depression she already had because of the loss of her husband," Jennifer said pleading for understanding.

"So, you decided to give this poor woman my baby… did it ever occur to you that I would have to face losing both my wife and my child? Did that ever enter that brain of yours?" Harry questioned.

"We really didn't have much time to think it through," Jennifer said.

"Are you saying that if you had time to think about it, you would have done it differently? You were Patricia's friend, you were my friend. And yet you deliberately made a decision that would affect many lives in the future. Karlah was also fed lies by her mother who, by the way, figured things out and confronted Mary about it, but continued to lie to Karlah. Lesley said Mary felt very guilty all these years. Did you ever feel guilty or even wonder about my little girl. When I begged you to have our child, did you think about where my little girl was or did you even have a conscience? I want you out of our lives. Sarah doesn't deserve a mother like you. With God as my witness, you will never be in her life again, I'll make sure of that," Harry said shaking.

Jennifer began to cry as she begged Harry for forgiveness. "Please, Harry, I am so sorry,"

"It's too late, you had all these years to come clean. I'm going to take you to the house and you are going to pack your things and move out," Harry said. Then he asked Sidney if he could leave Sarah here until he got back.

"Maybe Sarah could spend the night with the twins. I'm sure Annabelle and Jeffrey wouldn't mind," Sidney said calling Leslie on his cell phone.

Arrangements made for Sarah, Harry drove Jennifer, in silence, to their house and making sure she got all her things out of their bedroom and bathroom, he drove her to the Sheridan Hotel on Canal street and helped her carry her things to a room.

Molly Owen

"I will file for divorce first thing in the morning and with Annabelle's help, I'm sure I can get full custody of Sarah," he said before leaving her in the room. He then went back to his house and called Sidney to tell him it was all taken care of and he would talk to Annabelle the next day about filing for a divorce.

Harry sat on the side of his bed, exhausted mentally and emotionally. He bowed his head and began to talk to his heavenly father, *"Oh God, I'm so sorry I haven't kept you in my life, especially for Sarah. I know I must forgive Jennifer, but God, I just can't. Help me, Lord. Bring me some peace. And God, in all my anger I still ask that you be with Jennifer. As surprised as I was tonight. I know this was a shock for her, too. I don't hate her, Father, after all, she is my wife. But she was so wrong to do what she did. I think about the lost years with Karlah, and I get angry all over again. Lord, I ask that you take this anger from me, give me strength for the things I need to do. I think about Karlah's adopted mother and the burden she carried all these years and how hard it must have been to keep that secret from Karlah. Thank you, Father, for Karlah. She is a fine young woman, and I am proud to call her my daughter. Help us as we build this relationship and become a family. Oh God, help me explain everything to Sarah. I pray this in Jesus' Name. Amen."*

Chapter 30

Leslie took the phone off the receiver and put it to her ear. Looking through the glass at Nick, she realized that time had not been good to him. His face was covered in deep wrinkles, his eyes were sunken, surrounded by dark circles. He still had a full head of hair but it was almost white. The salt and pepper gray beard covered most of his lower face. The only thing that resembled the man she knew was his smile.

"Hi, Leslie. I hope everything is alright. I couldn't believe the guard when he told me I had a woman visitor. I'm really glad to see you."

"Everything's alright, Nick."

"I'm relieved. I was afraid it had to do with Ryan when I saw you sitting there. I couldn't think of a reason for you to come unless it was about Ryan," Nick said.

"Some things have been happening lately that made me realize that spur of the moment decisions can have a lasting effect on those we love the most. I want to have a relationship with you. I came today to ask your forgiveness, and to once again forgive you. What's in the past is over, but with our Lord's help, we can move on and build a common ground for both of us to stand on. Is that something you can see us doing?"

"Most assuredly. I've prayed for this for a long time, Leslie," Nick said smiling. "I want to tell you what a fine young man you have raised. You and Sidney have done a great job with that boy. Please forgive me for not being there to help your mother raise you."

"Thank you,"

"And, Leslie, I'm very proud of you and all you have accomplished. I asked Ryan to bring me the books you have written. I've read every one of them and I've learned many things from them about you. I'm sorry I wasn't there for you growing up and losing your mother. I'm sorry I wasn't the kind of father you would have picked. However, while here I have taught myself many things on many subjects. I read the Bible daily and I depend on God to see me through. I pray for you and Ryan every night before I go to sleep. I tell you all of this so you will know I have changed. I'm not the Nick you once knew," he said with tears in his eyes.

Leslie choked back the desire to cry as she listened to him tell of all the work he was doing to be a better person. She could see he had changed. She decided the next time he went to the parole board she would be there to back him up. They talked a while longer, then Nick thanked Leslie for coming, and Leslie promised to come see him more often.

"Does Ryan know you came?" he asked before going with the guard.

The Cookbook

"Not yet. But I plan on telling him about our visit. He'll be pleased, Nick," Leslie told him.

"Does he know why you didn't come to see me before?"

"Yes, but only recently," Leslie told him.

They said goodbye and Nick left her sitting with the phone still in her hand. She let the tears flow, not because she was sad, but because she was so glad he was okay and working hard to change. For the first time in her life, she felt like she had a father. Thinking about Karlah, she was sure that was the way she must feel also.

*****

That evening she told Sidney about her visit to Nick and how he appeared to have changed.

"Like a chameleon changing his colors?" Sidney said a little skeptical.

"I don't think so, if you mean he has changed on the outside but is the same on the inside. I believe he has really changed. He said he prays for me and Ryan every night, and he has read all of my books, Sid. He said it has helped him to know me better," Leslie told him.

"I'm glad, Les. When are you going to tell Ryan?"

"When he comes Friday. I hope he brings Karlah with him. It might be an opportunity to share this experience with both of them," she said. "Have you heard any more from Harry?"

"About what?"

"Anything. What's he doing about Jennifer, Sarah, Karlah?" she stated frustrated at Sidney's question.

"Sorry, I didn't mean to upset you. I think I'll go to bed early if you don't mind?"

"Sid, what's wrong?"

"I'm just tired. It's been a long day. Don't worry. I'm alright," he said.

"Sid, you would tell me if something is wrong, wouldn't you?"

Getting up he went to Leslie and gave her a kiss on the cheek, then heading for the staircase. "Nothing is wrong, and yes I would tell you. I love you. See you in the morning,"

Unable to sleep, Leslie got up early and went downstairs to put on a pot of coffee. She had stayed awake most of the night just making sure Sidney was okay. *No wonder he's tired. He has really been busy with this Harry thing. That's why he slept so soundly all night,* she thought. The pot stopped dripping and she poured out two cups, set them on a tray and climbing the back stairs she carried them to their bedroom.

She heard the water running in the shower and put a cup of coffee on the nightstand next to Sidney's side of the bed. Waiting for him to come out of the bathroom, she bowed her head and began to pray aloud *"Father, thank you for taking care of Sidney, and Lord, help me remember to see that he takes it easy. We are so grateful for the blessing you give our family every day. "Thank you, God, for keeping us in your sight. Thank you, Father, for Nick and for all his efforts in learning more about you. I pray you bless him and give him peace, Lord. I pray for Harry, Sarah, Karlah, and yes, God, I pray for Jennifer too. I pray Harry finds it in his heart to forgive her. Be with us today, Lord. Give us your grace through Jesus Christ our Savior, In His Name. Amen."*

"Amen," Sidney said coming into the bedroom.

The Cookbook

Lesley opened her eyes and looked at Sidney then smiled. "Are you feeling better," she asked, getting up and putting her arms around him, giving him a big hug.

"Yes, I am. Thanks for letting me sleep," he said picking up a cup of coffee. "And thanks for the coffee."

"Let's go eat some breakfast," she said putting the cups on the tray and handing it to Sidney as they went back downstairs to the kitchen.

Chapter **31**

Since it wasn't unusual for Jennifer to be out of town for a few days, Harry didn't have to explain anything to Sarah right away. He made arrangements with Karlah to have lunch after her classes on Wednesday. That gave him enough time to talk to Annabelle about legal questions.

Sitting across the desk from Annabelle, he was aware of how professional she was as she explained the procedure for filing divorce papers. As she explained each item she handed him a sheet of paper to sign. When it came to custody of Sarah, she told him that would be determined by the court.

"What about Jennifer's role in the deception?" he asked.

"That's a criminal matter that will be investigated by the police," she told him.

"Who will tell the police what happened?"

"It will probably come to light during the divorce proceedings," she said. "Have you talked to her about the divorce?"

"No. She is staying at the Sheridan. I haven't seen nor talked to her since I took her there the night I discovered what she had done," Harry told her.

"What about Karlah? Does she know the role Jennifer played in all of this?"

"I'm having lunch with her tomorrow. Do you think I should tell her everything? I was hoping we could just get to know each other."

"Don't you think she is going to want to know Sarah's reaction to the news that they are sisters?" Annabelle asked him.

"That's the other thing. It will be hard enough to tell her about Karlah and how that all happened, but I don't know how I am going to be able to tell her about her mother," he said.

"Harry, God will be with you. He will guide your words. You have a close relationship with Sarah and she trusts you. She will know that she can depend on you to keep her safe and protect her," Annabelle assured him. "I know that right now you are very angry with Jennifer but for Sarah's and Karlah's sake, your anger should take a back seat. They'll want you to be a rock, and they'll need you to include God in the conversations with them."

"Thank you, Annabelle. You are so right. I'll have to tell Karlah about Jennifer's role in all of this. That won't be easy either," Harry said shaking his head in despair.

"You have our support and we can help you with Sarah. Karlah is already facing many things, but she will also be able to help with Sarah because Sarah looks up to her. The fact that Karlah is her sister will help, giving her something else to think about," Annabelle said standing up and offering her hand.

"Thank you again for everything, Annabelle," Harry said shaking her hand.

"I'll be in touch. I'll let you know when the papers have been served to Jennifer. I'll say a prayer for you, Harry. With God's help it will work out for the best," she said walking him to the door of her office.

Annabelle went back to her desk and sitting down she bowed her head and prayed, *Father, Lord of all, be with Harry give him words for his daughter Sarah, help him remain compassionate as he deals with the hurt this will cause. Be with Sarah, God, she is just a little girl and this is a lot to take in, I love you God and I know you will give her peace through this. I ask you to give Karlah strength and courage to face this also. Thank you, Father, for your grace and your son Jesus Christ, in His name I pray. Amen.*

*****

Even though apprehensive about meeting with Harry alone, Karlah prepared herself and drove to the Café Royale on Royal in the French Quarter where he suggested they meet. Entering through the French doors she found him sitting in the corner facing her. When he saw her, he stood up and waved. As she approached the table he walked toward her and hesitated.

"May I give you a hug?" he asked

She nodded and they hugged briefly. Then helping her with her chair, he waited for her to sit down before sitting down across from her.

"Thank you for coming. I hope this isn't interfering with your classes," he said.

"No, but I had an important test this morning. I hope I did well on it. It's a good portion of my grade for this semester," she told him.

"I'm sure you did well … but in light of the circumstances, I hope you could study," he said.

"Ryan helped me, and I think I did okay. I'll soon find out," she said looking at the menu.

"He's a nice young man," he commented.

"Yes, and so are his parents," she said wondering why she felt the need to defend the Ryes.

They ordered and while waiting for their meal they began to talk more freely, taking turns sharing about their lives. He told her he was a stockbroker and was born and raised in the French Quarter but now he and his family lived in the Garden District not far from the Ryes. Then Harry asked her how she ended up teaching gymnastics and she told him about how Nancy had raised her as a single mom, and she was following in her footsteps.

"She did a good job raising you. You are a fine young lady and she would be proud of your accomplishments," he told her.

"Thank you. You've done a good job with Sarah. She is a sweet little girl and I can't wait for her to find out we are sisters," Karlah said taking a sip of ice tea, a little more relaxed in their conversation.

"I want to talk to you about that," Harry said putting his fork down and wiping his mouth with the napkin. "There is something you can help me with. I really don't know how to tell

The Cookbook

you this. My wife Jennifer was good friends with your mother Patricia. She is also a Realtor. That said, when your Aunt Mary… when she told you about everything, she mentioned a real estate lady encouraging her to switch the babies," he said.

Karlah sat very still listening intently to what he was trying to say. She could tell it was hard for him to talk about and then she began to understand.

"Are you saying your wife, Sarah's mother is the Realtor that Mary was talking about?"

Harry nodded his head and sat quietly waiting for the rest of it to sink in.

"I'm so sorry, Mr. Burke… Harry, how hard that must be for you," she said reaching across the table for his hand. "But, what can I help you with?"

"I have to tell Sarah,"

"Oh," she said taking her hand back and leaning back in her chair as she thought about Sarah and what affect this information could have on her.

"When I found out the truth about Jennifer, I told her to move out and I've filed for divorce. I haven't said anything to Sarah. Then I thought by telling her she now has a sister, it would soften the blow, so to speak," Harry continued.

"Were you going to tell her everything, the whole truth, including the part her mother played in it?" Karlah asks with concern.

"I don't know. I don't want her to have hard feelings about her mother, but she may find out later and blame me for not telling her the truth now," Harry told her.

Karlah thought about all the lies that she had lived with all these years and how it would affect Sarah if she found out much later. Karlah knew that the information she now had about the only mother she ever knew was a hard pill to swallow. But, she wasn't sure if she had known at Sarah's age, if it would have made a difference. Sarah's mother was still alive and she would have to deal with that along with knowing what she did, and why. It occurred to Karlah that there could be legal action, not only for Mary as a midwife, but for Jennifer's role in the deception.

"This will be a hard decision for you to make. I'll help you when the time comes to tell her but you have to decide what is best for her. Even though our circumstances are similar, they are not the same. She'll have to deal with her mother now, where I can't deal with the only mother I've ever known. Do you understand?" Karlah said realizing how difficult all of this had been for him.

"Yes, I understand what you're saying. This was difficult enough knowing that I lost all of those years with you, then to find out that my wife the mother of my child had something to do with it those many years ago... Well, I must admit I'm having a hard time with it. I'm so angry with Jennifer and Karlah I don't know if I can forgive her," he said.

"I understand how you feel. I told Mary that I thought her heart was in the right place, but I didn't know if I could forgive her for keeping me from my biological family. I hope someday you and I will be able to forgive."

"Unfortunately, Jennifer's motives were not honorable. I can almost accept Mary's role in this, she wanted to help her niece, but Jennifer only wanted to satisfy her own wants. I'm sorry, I just can't forgive her and I don't want Sarah influenced by her self-centeredness," Harry said.

The Cookbook

"Leslie, Ryan's mother, gave me a scripture to rely on. It's in Proverbs, I can't remember where the verse is but it says something like *trust God with all your heart and lean not on your own understanding.* This is what will get us through. We must trust in God," Karlah said in all sincerity looking at Harry. "I pray that someday we'll be able to forgive those who made poor decisions that affected our lives so drastically. I still find it hard to believe that they could do that and move on as if nothing had changed."

"Patricia would be so pleased to see how you have become such a wise person at such a young age. I hope you know how much I love you, and how proud I am to be your father," Harry said, choking up.

"On a happier note, I must get to the gym before my students get there. Are you going to bring Sarah today?"

"Oh yes. I almost forgot. You go ahead while I pay the bill and I'll see you later. And Karlah, thank you for coming. It's been good to get to know you better," he said giving her a quick hug.

The Cookbook

Chapter **32**

After much consideration, Leslie titled her first cookbook *'From Leslie's Garden.'* She was very pleased with the design on the cover from a local graphic designer and Pearl's stylizing for Leslie's photos were perfect. Now all the hard work coming up with recipes then testing them, photos of the finished product and historical information behind the vegetables and recipes were about to pay off. She was getting ready to send everything to the printer. After one more quick look, she sent the files off.

"So, I sent the files to the printer today and, in a few days, I'll have a proof copy. I'm so excited to see it in print," Leslie told Annabelle.

"I'm anxious to see the finished product," she said knowing how long Leslie had worked on it. "We'll have to celebrate when you get the proof."

"How are things going with you? Any new trials to keep you busy?" Leslie said.

"I'm waiting on a court date for Harry's divorce. Do you know if he has talked to Sarah about everything?"

"Karlah told Ryan that she and Harry were going to talk to Sarah together but she wasn't sure when. I think she's anxious to be able to tell Sarah they are sisters. She really loves that little girl. She and Harry have been together a couple of times getting to know each other and talk about their future as a family," Leslie shared.

"Speaking of Karlah. Did you notice her and Ryan holding hands at the prayer meeting? Are they an item now?" Annabelle asked.

"I think so. I just hope it doesn't interfere with their studies. With the end of the year in sight, this summer could accelerate their relationship. However, I've given it to God. If this is his plan, then I'll not stand in the way. I think Karlah is growing in her faith with Ryan's help and I'm pleased about that. He couldn't have picked a nicer girl if he tried, and we have spent enough time with her to evaluate that," Leslie told her.

"I agree with you wholeheartedly. I'm quite impressed with that young lady. On her own, she supports herself and goes to school. She must be commended for that. How is she doing with the rest of it? You know about her birth mother and Harry," Annabelle asked.

"Ryan says she is doing really well. Harry is helping her fill in blanks as far as his and Patricia's family is concerned and she has started a family tree with the DNA Company. You know before, she didn't have any idea who her family was, and that is why she sent for her DNA kit."

"Well, Leslie if this relationship lasts then you are very fortunate."

"Yes, we are. I still hope they wait and finish school before they get too serious," Leslie said. "That's just the mother in me talking."

"I know. Call me when the proof copy comes and we'll have lunch to celebrate," Annabelle said before they said goodbye.

The Cookbook

Chapter ***33***

Ever since the night Jennifer was exposed as the real estate lady that encouraged Mary to switch babies, she had stayed in Leslie's thoughts. There was something yet undiscovered about her, that tugged relentlessly at Leslie's heartstrings. In her research about Jennifer in connection with Harry's quest for the true identity of his daughter, she had discovered some things. Jennifer was the last of six children born into a family full of despair, her father died shortly after she was born, leaving her mother to support six children under the age of nine. Her older siblings raised the younger children while her mother worked for one of the more affluent families in the garden district. When Jennifer was fifteen, her mother had a nervous breakdown and Jennifer had to quit school to care for her. She struggled to get her GED and attended Community College while working for a real estate office as the receptionist. Leslie could see how resentment was a common trait as Jennifer determined to overcome everything she knew growing up.

Molly Owen

It was no wonder she strived to overcome her upbringing. She just wanted to be like the people her mother worked for. When Patricia died she suddenly saw an opportunity for a better life for herself and without hesitation, she took advantage of it. Leslie surmised.

Sidney had shared with Leslie that Harry, after the discovery of her role in switching the babies, had taken Jennifer to the Sheridan Hotel on Canal Street. Leslie was feeling a strong desire to go see her. Was it God telling her to go? *I could take the St. Charles Streetcar to Canal Street.* She thought. She would have to talk to Sidney about it. Now with the cookbook at the printer she had more time. Getting up from her desk she headed for the Studio.

"So, what do you think? Am I crazy for caring about her?" Leslie asked.

"No. I think you are being called to be there for her. It doesn't look like, from what you have told me, that she has anyone else. So I think you should follow your instincts. You have my permission," Sidney said with a wink.

"Well thank you, I think," she said laughing.

*****

Standing in the hall outside the door of the hotel room, she hesitated, then knocked and waited. She knocked again, still nothing. Starting to walk away, the door opened.

"Hello, Jennifer. It's Leslie. May I please come in?' Leslie said.

Jennifer backed away from the door waving her arm into the room indicating that she could come in as Leslie walked passed her. Jennifer, void of makeup with uncombed hair and still in her nightclothes, sat down at the end of the bed and Leslie sat in the chair across from her.

"So, what do you want?" Jennifer said.

"I just came to see how you are and if there is anything I can do for you," Leslie told her.

"You're kidding? Because of you and that husband of yours, my husband has kicked me out, and he's filed for divorce," Jennifer said.

Leslie stayed quiet while she let the words from Jennifer linger in the air hoping she would realize her own role in her situation. The silence was finally broken, and Jennifer started telling Leslie about her struggles to be somebody.

"Harry was my ticket out of my mediocre existence. All I wanted was to be like all of you… you know, the upper class. I worked hard in my job, but I wanted the prestige that comes from wealth, the kind you and Annabelle have. I didn't deliberately start out to hurt Harry. I didn't know he wanted children. That was the last thing I wanted. I looked at my mother, and thought no man is going to keep me pregnant so that I can't be anything but a baby factory. I didn't want to have Sarah, but Harry wouldn't let it rest. So, I finally gave in. But, only if he would take care of her and let me have my career. That's what we agreed on. Now he has Karlah. Karlah? How ironic is that? I still can't believe it. And, how on earth did you find that midwife? I just can't win. That's what I mean, Leslie, this is the story of my life," Jennifer said.

"I do understand Jennifer, however sometimes when we let our life's bad experiences take control of our actions, we find we have to pay the consequences. That's when we feel nothing is going our way, when in fact, we're responsible for our reactions. You're not alone in your negative reaction to events in your previous life. I, along with others that you admire so much, have skeletons that we've had to overcome. I believe the only difference in our reactions and yours, is our relationship with God," Leslie said seeing Jennifer's expression change as she was ready to defend herself.

"Before you dismiss this observation, ask yourself this question. Would my life be better with God in it? And remember all the hard things you have had to face alone, were when God didn't exist in your life," Leslie continued.

Jennifer didn't say anything. She thought about what Leslie was saying. She was on the defense and wanted to justify her actions according to her own understanding, but for some reason, what Leslie had said was starting to make sense. Not ready to take responsibility for anything, she countered with her own reasoning.

"Yes, but I bet that is the way you were raised. I've never gone to church and I don't know this God you are talking about. If he does exist, then why does he let these things happen? Why does he let people like me get into trouble? Why did he take away my father? I never even knew him. Why did this God of yours do that to me? Wasn't I good enough for this God of yours?"

"Those are very good questions, Jennifer. Believe it or not, I've had doubts about God and I've asked Him why. We, as Christians, are human, Jennifer, and we hurt when bad things happen to us just like everyone else, but the difference is that we know God loves us and forgives our sins. He loves us so much, Jennifer, that he gave his Son, Jesus Christ, to die on the cross for our sins. His love for us is above any love we could ever experience," reaching into her purse Leslie told her. "I brought you something," Handing her the Bible she saw tears in

The Cookbook

Jennifer's eyes as she saw her name engraved in gold on the front of the wine-colored leather.

"I've never seen my name in gold on anything and I've never had my own Bible. There is one on the table by the bed in this room but I never opened it," she said, choking back tears.

"I'll be happy to help you understand what you read to the best of my ability. Perhaps later, we can study it together. I understand your world is upside down right now and it won't be easy to get back in the swing of things. But you'll feel better after you've had a shower and gotten dressed. Then you will be able to face the outside again. When you take Jesus as your Savior things will change for the better. You can trust me when I tell you that. Just remember, that God is there for you. Talk to Him, cry with Him, laugh with Him, He is a good listener, and He will help you. I left my cell number on a card inside your Bible," she said getting up and walking toward the door with Jennifer following her.

"Thank you, Leslie, for putting my name on the Bible," she said not yet understanding what this visit would mean for her future. After shutting the door, she flipped some of the pages in the bible and laid it down on the bed. Sitting in the chair across from it, she stared at her name engraved in gold and wondered what was in this book that would help her. Leslie was right, her world was up-side-down, but she didn't think reading this book of foreign words was going to help her with Harry.

Chapter 34

Walking hand in hand around the square in front of the St. Louis Cathedral, Sidney squeezed Leslie's hand, then looking at her, he smiled. They had just celebrated the printing of her first cookbook at Brennen's where they had a romantic dinner. He reminded her of the time during their courtship when he treated her to a surprise at Brennen's.

"I remember. It was after a book signing. I almost missed the plane and I couldn't wait to get back to New Orleans to see you," she said.

"I was head over heels in love with you Leslie LaRue," he told her. "It's a beautiful day, and I'm spending it with the love of my life. Thank you for being my wife."

"Stop it, Sid. You're going to make me cry," she said leaning on his shoulder.

Molly Owen

"Look, Les. Let's have our caricature done with both of us," he said pulling her by the hand toward the artist. "We can frame it and put it next to the caricature of you in my office."

Sitting in front of the artist brought back memories of that day long ago when she and Sidney first got acquainted. She thanked God for their many years of marriage and for their son, Ryan. They were truly blessed and no matter the daily routine they always remembered to thank God for the many blessings He bestowed on them.

Soon the artist was finished and handed them the results. They both laughed when they saw the finished product. Thanking the artist, they rolled it up and Sidney put it under his arm as they continued to walk around the square.

Everywhere they looked, merchants were getting ready for Mardi Gras which was coming soon. The big event of the year took much preparation and it took over the French Quarter from Bourbon Street to the French Market by the river.

"Do you think Karlah will end up being our daughter-in-law?" Leslie asked as they stepped off the sidewalk to avoid a group of people looking at an artist rendition of the French Quarter.

"It seems to be getting serious, alright," he said. "I'm okay with it. But I do wish they would wait a while. However love doesn't always follow life's schedule, does it?" he said winking at Lesley.

They stopped to watch as street performers, mimes, jugglers and musicians treated people from the steps of the cathedral with their talents. It had been a wonderful day spent carefree just the two of them as they headed back to catch the streetcar that would take them home. Sidney helped Leslie climb the steps while they found a seat close to the back of the

The Cookbook

car. There was a slight breeze and Sidney put his arm around her shoulders to help her keep warm. When they left the car on St. Charles Ave they walked a couple of blocks to their home. Entering the house, Leslie went to the kitchen to make some coffee while Sidney closed and locked the front door, then joined her in the kitchen.

"Thank you for a great day, Sid, we should do this more often," she said turning the coffee pot on.

"You are very welcome, Mrs. Rye, and you're right, let's do this more often," he said, giving her a hug.

Leslie's cell phone began to buzz. Reaching into her pocket, she looked at the screen. "It's Annabelle."

"Hello," Leslie said.

"Hi, I don't want to keep you. I just wanted to give you a heads up. Harry's divorce was finalized today, and he was awarded full custody of Sarah," Annabelle told her.

"That's great," Leslie said.

"That's not all. It came out in Harry's reason for asking for divorce that Jennifer was an accessory to the crime committed by Mary and they are both being arrested on those charges first thing in the morning."

"So soon?"

"Yes, the Judge took a real interest in what Harry told the court and wanted an arrest warrant for both Jennifer and Mary done immediately."

"I wonder if Harry is going to warn Jennifer," Leslie said remembering her visit with Jennifer.

"I wouldn't think so. He's still pretty angry with her. And Leslie I don't blame him."

"Oh, I don't either. I didn't tell you but I went to see her the other day. I felt called to give her some hope. I took her a Bible. I think with some encouragement she could turn to God. I know what she did was wrong and I'm not defending her but she has never had God in her life and I'm hoping she'll start to look for answers in the Bible," Leslie said while Sidney listened and nodded his head in agreement.

Chapter **35**

Laughter and squealing exploded from the room and could be heard down the hall in her dorm. The three of them looked at each other with tears running down their faces from the laughing.

"When daddy said we were going to college to see Karlah, well I was very confused and wondered why, but now I know, and I'm so excited. I always wanted a sister, but mom just brushed it off every time I brought it up. But, now I have a big sister, and I already love her," Sarah said hugging Karlah so hard she almost knocked her over.

Joy filled his heart as Harry sat watching his girls enjoy each other laughing hugging dancing around. As things began to calm down, he wondered if Sarah would start asking questions. She seemed to accept what Karlah told her without any concern with why. He wasn't going to push her. He would wait until she was ready to hear the answers.

Karlah simply told Sarah that recently she had discovered that Harry was her father, and that made them sisters. All Sarah heard was that they were sisters. She was still leaning on Karlah when her mind went to why was her dad Karlah's father.

"Is Mom your mother?" Sarah said.

"No. My mother was your dad's first wife. She died when I was born and I was raised by my adopted mother," Karlah said quite matter-of-factly.

"Oh," She said.

Karlah looked at Harry and smiled, letting him know she thought things were going well. He smiled back in agreement.

"Ryan is coming over soon. Why don't we all go out for lunch? What do you say?"

"Oh, yes. Can we, Dad?"

"Yes, I think that's a good idea. I understand that you and Ryan help in Leslie's garden on Saturdays. So, after lunch maybe we can go with you and help also," Harry said.

*****

Not wanting to shed a bad light on Sarah's mother, Harry explained that he and Jennifer would get a divorce, and Sarah would live with him. Her mom could come to see her but she would no longer live with them. The reason for all the changes in her life didn't seem to bother Sarah right now, although he was sure, as she grew older, she would have questions that he would have to prepare himself to answer. However, for now, she was satisfied with what she knew and the fact that Karlah was now her big sister was uppermost in her mind. He felt bad about the fact that she didn't seem worried that her mom wouldn't be around. But he knew that

The Cookbook

was Jennifer's choice, not to participate in Sarah's life. In one respect the very fact that she wasn't a mainstay in Sarah's life, made it easier not only for Sarah, but also for himself

Chapter 36

While Sidney showered and dressed for the day Leslie went down to start their breakfast. She put a CD of contemporary Christian music that Ryan gave her for her birthday in the CD player to listen to while she prepared the batter for waffles. Humming to one of the songs, she felt Sidney's arms around her waist.

"Is that one of the songs on that CD Ryan gave you?" he said moving to the cabinet and getting out dishes for the waffles.

"Yes. It has a very good message. Have you heard it?" she asked.

"No I haven't but I would like to hear it. Can we play it again?" he said restarting the player.

Leslie's Cell phone began to ring. Trying to remove the waffles from the waffle iron she motioned for Sidney to answer it.

"Hello," Sidney said holding Leslie's cell phone.

"Hold on, where are you? Yes. We'll be right there. Where is Sarah? Okay, okay, we're coming."

"What?" Leslie said turning off the waffle iron.

"That was Harry. He's at the hospital. Jennifer tried to commit suicide," Sidney said putting the dishes back in the cabinet.

"Is she okay?"

"Yes, she called him after she took the pills. When he got to the hotel room she was unconscious, and he called 911. The operator told him to walk her around until they got there. He saw the Bible with her name on it. Then, at the hospital, he saw your cell number on the card you put in the Bible while he waited for word of her condition. I guess that's why he called. Come on let's go," Sidney said.

When they got to the hospital they found Harry in the waiting room. He sat with his head down in his hands. They walked up to him. He looked up and shook his head.

"I never thought she would do anything like this. She's always been so in control. I know she wasn't happy about the divorce and Sarah, but honestly, I thought she would just move on like she did when giving my daughter away. This isn't like her at all," Harry told them.

"Did anything else happen?" Leslie said remembering what Annabelle had told them earlier.

"Not that I know of," he answered.

"Were you aware that the authorities were going to serve her with a warrant for her arrest this morning?" Sidney said.

"No. But how would she know that?" Harry said confused.

"That's a good question, Sidney," Leslie said. "If you don't mind, I think I'll head for the Buck Farm." Looking at Harry "They'll arrest Mary this morning and I think Ben will need someone there."

"Harry, I need to go with Leslie. We'll be back and you can keep us updated. I'll call Jeffrey and let him know what's going on," Sidney said. "But before we go, let's say a prayer together," Sidney said taking Harry and Leslie's hands. *"Heavenly, Father, You are an awesome God, a healing God we praise you, Father, for all the blessings you have given us. We ask you to be with Jennifer, give her hope, peace, and strength as she fights her way back. Be with Harry, show him Your everlasting love, God. Bring him peace and understanding as he deals with many emotions and thoughts during this latest development in his life. And, Heavenly Father, we ask you to be with Sarah. They all three need You, Father. Thank you, for giving them strength and courage for what's ahead. In Jesus' Name, we pray. Amen."*

"Thanks for coming and for your prayers, Sidney. And Leslie, thank you for the Bible you gave to Jennifer. I hope she will be able to learn from it," he said more confused now that Leslie wanted to go to the Buck Farm.

Chapter 37

Arriving at the Buck farm, they saw them taking Mary into custody. She and Sidney got out of the car and walked toward Ben. His face was sad and confused all at the same time. Leslie explained what had happened. Telling him the results of the research. He began shaking his head in denial

"She was following her heart, Leslie, she meant no harm," Ben said.

"However, Ben, she didn't consider the consequences of her actions, and that's unacceptable. Lives have been nearly destroyed by her rash decision. A father lost time with his child. A child grew up not knowing her father. Can't you see the harm she has done?"

"I can, but I know my sister, and you would think the good she has done with many women throughout the years would make up for one wrong," he said.

"Maybe her motives were in the right place. However, her actions were far from right. Can you understand the pain she inflicted on two families? Would it not have been better to suffer the truth at the time and possibly give a chance for other children and perhaps even another spouse and more children for her niece? She was still young and had a lifetime ahead of them. Did your sister discount the father's role in this?" Leslie said in anger.

With tears in his eyes, he watched as they took away his sister. He knew Leslie was right, but he loved his sister and didn't want her to go to jail.

"What about the real estate lady? What will happen to her?" Ben questioned.

"Her part in all of this by encouraging Mary in the deception made her an accessory to a criminal act. She may spend time in jail, but because of her sins, her husband has divorced her and he is getting full custody of their twelve-year-old daughter. She will always have to live with what she has done to them," Leslie told him.

"Ben, pray for your sister. We'll pray for you both. As hard as this is for you and Mary, God knows your pain and he will be there for both of you," Leslie said giving him a hug.

Sidney shook Ben's hand and they walked back to the car. As they drove down the road leaving the farm, Leslie looked back at her friend.

"It's just so sad," she said watching Ben stand in the middle of the yard in front of the farmhouse like a lost little boy.

"It reminds us that the decisions we make can affect us for the rest of our lives. Those same decisions can also change the lives of other people. Especially when made in haste and

The Cookbook

without consideration of others. Even the best of intentions can harm others, sometimes we aren't even aware of the harm it has done. I wonder if Mary, or Nancy for that matter, were even aware that there was a father involved?"

"That's why prayer is so important, Sid. A good faithful relationship with Jesus, our Savior, is the foundation that guides us. We aren't perfect and we make mistakes but with God by our side, we can be forgiven," Leslie said bowing her head in silent prayer as she asked for God's presence in the lives of everyone affected by this turn of events.

"Jennifer is awake and talking. So she'll be alright," Leslie said reading from her cell phone text.

"She'll have therapy, I'm sure, and it will be a long haul for her but I'm glad she is okay," Sidney said.

"Yes, and for Harry and Sarah too," Leslie said. *"Thank you, Father, for answered prayers."*

"Amen."

Chapter 38

Sitting across the table from, Sidney, she felt a surge of deep love for her husband. "Thank you, Sid, for loving me, and for marrying me, and giving me a son. I don't tell you often enough, but I love you so very much," she said with tears in her eyes.

Sidney looked at her and smiled. "You are the best thing that ever happened to me, Les. I mean that. I think about life without you and I can't imagine what it would be like. You are a wonderful wife, mother, friend and I appreciate you more than you will ever know," he told her reaching across the table for her hand.

After they finished their meal, they cleared the table and began to clean the kitchen side by side.

"We make a good team, you and I," Sidney said drying a dinner plate and returning it to the cabinet.

"Yes. I'm so sorry for Harry. I'm sorry he couldn't have what we have, especially for his daughters," Leslie said turning off the water.

Putting the dish towel down, Sidney took Leslie into his arms. "God has blessed us, Leslie. We must never forget that," he said giving her a big hug. "How about you and I go to the French Quarter. It's still early, we can walk around the square or go into the art galleries or whatever you feel like doing. What do you say?"

"I say great idea. Let's do it. Maybe we can stop at La Madelyn's for a cup of java like we used to do," she answered.

They took a taxi to the square in front of the St. Louis Cathedral. The weather was nearly perfect, with a slight breeze coming in from the river and there were many people out and about enjoying the evening. They crossed the street and went into a millinery shop to look at hats.

"Hi, Mom, Dad," Ryan said. "What are you two doing here?"

"Probably the same as you two. Enjoying the beautiful weather," Leslie said giving Karlah a hug.

"Don't you just love this place?" Karlah said, taking a hat off the hat stand and trying it on.

"Hey, that looks really good on you," Ryan said. "I'm not kidding. How much is it?"

"Ryan, I can't buy this hat. Where would I wear it?" she said.

"You could start a trend. Maybe wear it to a prayer meeting. We could buy one for Sarah and you both could start a trend together?" Ryan said.

"Now you're being silly," Karlah said putting the hat back on the hat stand.

"We are headed for the Bakery if you care to join us for coffee and dessert?" Sidney said

"Like a double date," Leslie said winking at Ryan.

"We would love to," Karlah said taking Ryan's hand.

Following the young people down the sidewalk, he gave Leslie a smile and a wink then took her hand in his. The four stopped in front of the shops and peered into the windows. Eventually, they came to the Bakery and went inside. Finding a table, Leslie and Karlah sat down across from each other.

"So what are we in the mood for tonight, ladies?" Sidney asked standing next to Ryan by the table.

"I'll just have decaf and a slice of the buttermilk pie," Leslie said turning to Karlah.

"Well, I think I'll have a scone and a cup of cocoa," Karlah said.

When the men left to get their orders, Leslie asked Karlah how Harry and Sarah were doing.

"Harry is still upset about Jennifer. Did you know she's in a hospital getting much-needed therapy?"

"Yes, I've visited her a couple of times," Leslie said.

"She evidently has some real issues. I feel for Harry. I understand how hard it is, however he is staying positive for Sarah," Karlah told her.

"Did he tell Sarah anything?" Leslie asked.

"Only that Jennifer is sick and will be gone for awhile. She already knew about the divorce before Jennifer took all of those pills. We never did figure out how she got them. Ryan has really been a rock for me, Leslie. I don't know what I would do without him. He keeps me grounded. You and Sidney did a wonderful job raising him," she said a little embarrassed, realizing she was letting Leslie know how much she and Ryan meant to each other.

"Thank you. And Karlah, Nancy did a good job raising you," Leslie said letting the feeling of concern that things were getting serious, pass.

"I've come to terms with what Nancy did and try to remember the good parts. I still regret the lost time with my father. But like Harry said, without everything that happened I wouldn't have a sister. I do love Sarah. It's strange how we connected the first time we met," Karlah shared.

"God always has a plan. He makes sure good things come, if we believe in him and accept His will to be done. He gives us so many blessings, some we are not even aware of, but he's always there watching over us," Leslie said just as Ryan and Sidney came back to the table.

"Here we go ladies," Sidney said setting the food on the table.

"Thank you," Leslie and Karlah said in unison.

"So how are things in the academic world? Are you two able to keep up with studies okay?" Sidney asked.

"Actually, we are both right on target," Ryan said winking at Karlah. "We study together most of the time, which works out great. We still are able to spend time together without hurting our studies," he said reassuring his parents.

"We are very proud of you both for keeping up your studies. We know having a relationship when you are in college can be stressful. But you seem to be handling both very well," Leslie said. "Not to mention other events you are dealing with."

"Thanks, Mom. I know you and Dad worry about us, but we are okay and we will soon have a year behind us," Ryan said. "We are both going to take some classes this summer and maybe some online classes as well."

"Sounds like a plan," Sidney said, thinking about the fact that they seem to be planning their future together.

"Karlah is moving out of the dorm, to save money, and moving in with Harry and Sarah," Ryan said. "And I have been thinking about asking you if I could move in with you this summer?" he finished.

"I don't see any problem with that. Were you planning on living on campus next year?" Leslie asked.

"Maybe," Ryan answered not wanting to think that far ahead, yet.

Soon the four were back out on the sidewalk telling each other goodbye as each couple went separate directions. Ryan and Karlah, holding hands went towards the French Market where Ryan had parked his truck. Both aware of the concerns that Leslie and Sidney had, and yet not deterred from their plans for the future, they turned and smiled at each other in agreement knowing what the other's thoughts were.

After taking Karlah back to the dorm, Ryan returned to the French Quarter, parked and walked back to the French Market where he went down the isles until he reached the jewelry vendors.

"Good evening, Ryan. How are you doing tonight?"

"Hello, I just want to make a payment on my layaway," Ryan said.

"Sure enough, let me find the card," the vendor told him. "Here it is, well, not much left on this. Do you want to pay it off?"

"Not yet," Ryan said. "Maybe next month," he told him.

"Very well then. You'll have one more payment and it's all yours," he said.

"Thank you," Ryan said taking the receipt.

So next month I'll ask Karlah to marry me and give her the ring, he thought. He knew his parents would be concerned but he and Karlah had a plan for their future and they were very much in love. They started out as friends and before they realized it, they were falling in love. He knew his mom and dad liked Karlah and she liked them, so their acceptance would come once they got passed the fact that they were still young. They planned to finish up their second year before getting married, then with help from Harry and Ryan's parents on tuition they could live in the married quarters while finishing their degrees.

*****

After leaving Ryan and Karlah, they went to find a taxi for their ride home. As they walked through the streets of the French Quarter, they shared their thoughts about the two young people. Leslie expressed how much they liked Karlah and if Ryan planned on marrying her, she was happy that they had found each other.

"They make a sweet couple and you can tell they are in love," she said.

"Yes, it sure looks like we may be getting a daughter," Sidney said squeezing Leslie's hand.

"If that's going to happen in the near future, we can help them, can't we?"

"If that's what they want?"

"Young love, how exciting," she said, remembering their own young love.

Sidney helped Leslie get into the taxi and shut the door. He went around and got in beside her. As the taxi pulled away and into the traffic Sidney leaned over and took Leslie in his arms and kissed her.

"Mature love is also pretty exciting if you ask me," he said.

Leslie, with a deep sigh, smiled and said, "it certainly is."

Another Beginning

GLOSSARY OF CAJUN CUISINE

Beignet (baan-yay) a French donut without a hole, sprinkled with powdered sugar and served warm

Boudin (boo-dahn) sausage made with meat, rice, Cajun seasoning, and green onions sometimes served with breakfast

Chayote (chai-ow-te) also known as mirliton squash, a succulent green pear-shaped tropical fruit belonging to the gourd family, that grows on vines and resembles cucumber in flavor, used in salad dressing at Thanksgiving in New Orleans

Étouffée (a-too-fay) coming from a French word meaning 'to smother,' it's a thick Cajun stew made with very little water, no roux, lots of peppers, onions and sometimes tomatoes

Filé (fee-lay) is a seasoning made from the ground, dried leaves of the sassafras tree, an integral part of Creole cooking, and is used to thicken and flavor Gumbos and other Creole dishes

Gumbo (gum-bow) made with a roux, Cajun Holy Trinity (onions, celery, and green peppers) and any kind of meat from chicken to shrimp, add water to the roux to make a thick soup, serve in a deep bowl with rice. Add file seasoning at the end when served. NOTE: don't use file seasoning if gumbo is made with okra

Jambalaya (jam-ba-lie-ya) a sort of stew with any kind of meat from poultry to game and fish or a combination of some, then combined with vegetables. It is a good dish for using refrigerator leftovers

Pain Perdu (pan-purdue) a French word meaning 'lost bread' Made with day-old bread sometimes raisins or cinnamon then dipped in milk and egg mixture with vanilla and fried in oil or butter. Served with syrup, butter, preserves or jams or sprinkled with powdered sugar

Mascarpone (maa-skaar-pow-nei) cheese close to clotted cream in taste. Made using cream cheese, sour cream, heavy whipping cream, and lemon. Use as a spread on toast, bagels, and toppings for desserts.

Mirepoix (meer-pwah) a flavor base in French cooking made from diced onion, celery, and carrots cooked in butter or oil on low heat for a long time to sweeten ingredients such as soups, sauces for meats, and marinades

Mirliton (mur-luh-tn) also called chayote or Jerusalem artichokes a squash-like pear-shaped light green fruit used in salads and in New Orleans at Thanksgiving in dressings or added to stews.

Roux (roo) a thickening for many dishes made with butter or oil and flour. A dark roux is cooked until it turns dark whereas a light roux is like a white sauce.